NI

Maggie Pearson lives in a ...... century cottage in Suffolk. She has worked as a librarian, barmaid, au pair, and freelance journalist, but mostly as a mother. Now that her three sons are grown-up, she is a full-time writer. Her first book for Hodder, *Owl Light*, was a W H Smith Mind Boggling Book.

Other Hodder titles:

Owl Light
Maggie Pearson

Companions of the Night
Vivian Vande Velde

Look for me by Moonlight
Mary Downing Hahn

The House of Birds
Jenny Jones

Daughter of Storms
Louise Coooper

Hauntings
Susan Price

Night People

Maggie Pearson

Hodder
Children's
Books

a division of Hodder Headline plc

A Catalogue record for this title is available
from the British Library

ISBN 0 340 68076 8

Typeset by Hewer Text Composition Services, Edinburgh
Printed and bound in Great Britain by
Cox & Wyman Ltd, Reading, Berks

Hodder Children's Books
A Division of Hodder Headline PLC
338 Euston Road
London NW1 3BH

For all the jazz bands who brightened up my teenage years.

Why, this is hell, nor am I out of it.
Thinkst thou that I, that saw the face of God,
And tasted the eternal joys of heaven,
Am not tormented with ten thousand hells,
In being deprived of everlasting bliss?

Christopher Marlowe, *Dr Faustus.*

CHAPTER ONE

Sometimes she still gets the feeling he's not far away, like a melody half heard and half remembered. A still figure glimpsed among scurrying crowds; a pale face caught for a second by the dancing disco lights. Walking down dark, empty streets, she hears his footsteps echoing behind her and she hurries on, afraid to stop and turn to find there's no one there.

Sometimes, when the loneliness gets too hard to bear, she even tries to conjure him out of light and shadows, like the first time she saw him, his face unnaturally pale and in his dark hair highlights glowing red as hell-fire.

She knew then that after all the years of running she'd come to the place where she was meant to be.

*　　*　　*

All her life they seemed to have been running away. She'd wake up one morning to find Chas with their gear ready packed.

'Come on,' he'd say. 'Time we moved on.'

And she'd scramble into her clothes, small fingers fumbling with buttons and laces, grabbing a crust of bread and the last of the milk. She soon learned not to ask questions. Where are we going? What's wrong with here? Why do we have to go *now*? Better to save her breath so she could keep up, taking two – three – steps to each one of his, so he wouldn't have to carry her as well as their bags and baggage. Always moving on. Flitting from landlords when they couldn't pay the rent. Slipping out from under the noses of the DSS hounds when Chas had been working cash-in-hand, so they could afford to keep warm as well as eat.

For a while they were on the run from the Law as well, when Grandma tried to get her taken into care on the grounds that Chas wasn't a fit father.

It must have been in Grandma's house that they lived at the very beginning. All Jools could remember was the lush pile carpet, thick enough for creepy-crawlies to get lost in, live out their lives and die

2

still searching for the way out. And a bath like a huge pink seashell curving round her. But there were always angry voices, shouting at one another. Even when they weren't speaking, they still went on shouting in their heads.

So one day Chas packed their stuff and they left, joining a bunch of travellers heading west, towards Glastonbury, and she was swept up into a living, loving, ever-changing web of brothers and sisters, aunts, uncles and cousins, dogs, chickens and goats and one pig. By day Chas worked at fruit-picking, busking, washing dishes, selling ice cream, serving on market stalls, whatever. At night the whispering dark wrapped itself around them, keeping them safe. She'd never been afraid of the dark, only of the dawn. It was at dawn that the heavies moved in, with dogs and riot gear, smashing the windows of the buses, scattering the family, driving them out, and Lady Rachel, half gypsy, half sixties flower-child, lost the baby she was expecting and was never the same again.

After that, it was mostly just the two of them, living in squats and bed-and-breakfasts and on council estates where the most vigorous form of life was the mould creeping up the walls.

Sometimes, when Chas got a gig, she'd curl up to sleep on the floor of some muso's bed-sit, in a haze of hand-rolled smoke, soft music guiding her down the road to dreamland. The sweetest jazz in all the world is played at four in the morning, when the punters have all gone home to their beds.

Soon they'd be moving on again. Always moving on. Until they came to this place. And she suddenly realised that they hadn't been running away at all. Without knowing it, all this time, they'd been running towards something. What that something was, was still a mystery.

It was just a small town like dozens of others they'd passed through. The artic driver who'd given them their last lift dropped them at a roundabout on the bypass. From there they walked.

They planned to look up an old mate, a bassist called Albie. Money was tight, as usual, so they didn't phone ahead. Bad move. Whoever gave them Albie's new address clean forgot to mention that he'd turned respectable since they saw him last, got himself a day-job and a mortgage, a wife – the lovely Brenda – and a sour-faced baby. Ten months old and already he'd made up his mind about the world. He didn't like it. On top of that, they seemed to have walked into the middle of a family row.

'Hey, Brenda!' yelled Albie. 'Look who's here! It's Chas and Jools.'

(Chas and Jools. They sounded like a music-hall turn, thought Jools, but she could live with it.)

'Oh yes?' said Brenda, about as welcoming as if they'd been doorstepping double-glazing. 'Tell them they can't stay.'

'Just so Chas can sign on, eh?' wheedled Albie. 'They can have the spare room.'

'You've got to decorate that before my mother comes.'

'I can't start till Friday, can I?'

'We'll give you a hand,' offered Chas. 'Have it done in no time.'

Brenda looked at him as if he was something she'd just scraped off her shoe. 'Till Friday, then,' she said. 'Tell them they've got to be out by Friday.'

They went to stow their gear in a poky little room.

These days Albie was keeping the double-bass down at the pub. Brenda wouldn't let him practise at home. She said it upset the baby.

A born sociopath, a shrew for a mother *and* a tin ear! Life had not been kind to Albie junior. 'Look at it this way,' Jools told him. 'Things can only get better from now on.'

He stared at her while he chewed over this idea. Then he started to bawl. Perhaps he knew something she didn't.

'Come on,' sighed Albie. 'I'll take you down the Spotted Cow.'

Halfway down the road, they could still hear the sprog yelling.

'If I could just teach him to carry a tune,' said Albie philosophically, 'I'd have a Rock Legend in the making.'

The Spotted Cow was one of those Edwardian places, all curlicues and stained-glass windows, which still managed to keep its dignity in spite of the tacky little pizza takeaway squashed up against it on one side and the second-hand furniture warehouse on the other.

At first glance there seemed to be a surprising number of customers inside, considering the time of day. Then Jools realised it was just the three of them and Josie, the landlady. The rest was all done by mirrors. Mirrors everywhere, volleying images back and forth. She came out of the ladies' and met her own reflection going in. Movement all around, in the mirrors and in their curved borders and in the polished brass and chrome: ghosts of years gone by still trapped and Josie's doppelgänger, in a big hat and feather boa, silently leading the company in the chorus of some old music-hall song.

Here, in a cupboard in the back room, languished the true love of Albie's life, Samantha. She might be just a lump of wood with strings attached, but she had fantastic curves and together they made sweet music.

It seemed only right to let the two of them have a private moment together. Chas left the clarinet on the bar and went to see what sort of a tune he could get out of the old piano in the corner. He tried out a riff of this and that, isolating the duff notes. It wasn't long before he had the lid open and his head inside, one hand still fingering the keys.

After a while he surfaced again and strolled over to the bar. 'I could fix that for you, if you like,' he told Josie.

Josie looked doubtful. 'What will it cost me?'

Chas shrugged. 'Pay me in kind.'

'Depends what kind you had in mind,' said Josie, casually resting her 38D cups on the bar.

Jools could never work out what it was about Chas and women. Tall, dark and handsome he was not. At one time she used to think it must be the mothering instinct: *Poor guy! All alone in the world, with a little girl to look after.* As the little girl got bigger, Jools had done her best to blend into the woodwork while he did his stuff. It was only lately that she'd come to realise she didn't enter into it at all.

Chas had soon fixed himself up with a job helping behind the bar on Friday and Saturday nights. He went back to tinkering with the piano as another customer came in, wearing a battered top hat and a long patchwork coat of silks and satins in all the colours of the rainbow, and carrying a concertina.

Jools guessed he would have been about her own age, though it was hard to tell with black boys – they could often pass for older. Josie gave him the benefit and a pint of lager. 'Thirsty work, eh, Joseph? Busking.'

'Yep.' As he reached down into one of the coat's long pockets for some money, the head of a wooden marionette peeped out of the other with a cheeky grin.

Jools found herself grinning back.

Joseph glanced over at Chas. 'Getting the old joanna fixed at last?' he asked Josie.

'I'm working on it,' she said.

He gave her the thumbs-up, then took his drink and wandered over to talk to Chas. Soon he was sitting at the piano, fingering the keys. Albie brought Samantha in from the back room to join them. Chas fetched his clarinet from where he'd left it on the bar and the three of them started to jam. Nothing too flash, 'Carolina Moon', 'The Entertainer'. Every now and then, the piano would strike a bum note, but it still sounded pretty good. Josie hummed along as she emptied ashtrays and wiped down the tables.

All around, the ghosts in the mirrors danced to a different tune. Jools sat alone and forgotten, watching the ice dissolve in her tonic water. She fished out the slice of lemon and bit into it, savouring the sharp-sweet taste. That, at least, was real.

Always cultivate your pub landlady. She's the nearest Nature's come to inventing the Internet. Within two days, Josie had found a full-time job for Chas and a place for them both to stay. 'There's your new landlord. Over there.' She nodded. 'The port-and-lemon by the wall.'

Like a bottled spider, was the phrase that came to Jools' mind. Where did she get it from? *Richard III*? It just seemed to fit. Not that he was a hunchback or anything. His body was more the shape of an egg. He sat with his little legs dangling, not quite reaching the floor. And his arms, too, dangled, perfectly still, not touching the drink on the table beside him. Only his eyes moved, behind his John Lennon glasses, watching the world in mild surprise as if he'd discovered it newly hatched when he stepped out of his door that evening and was waiting to see what it would do next. The really creepy thing about him was that he seemed to have picked out the one spot in the room not covered by the mirrors. There wasn't a single reflection of him anywhere.

Chas took his drink and strolled over, introduced himself to the old man and sat down, while Jools stayed at the bar with Josie.

'Who is he?' asked Jools.

'The Prof? Says he's writing a book. Has been ever since I've known him.'

One of those books that never get finished. The world's full of them.

Then duty called Josie away to the other end of the bar where a bunch of weary travellers were dying of thirst, and Jools was left wondering what sort of work the Prof had to offer. If he was looking for an assistant to help him keep his notes in order, and so on, he'd come to the wrong place. Chas couldn't find a matching pair of socks without her help.

She strained her ears but she couldn't make out a word that passed between them, until the old man suddenly lifted his voice so the whole bar could hear, 'I cannot be doing with women,

11

you understand!' which turned a few heads besides hers.

Then Chas called her over and the Prof stared thoughtfully at her through his glasses as if she was some kind of specimen he'd got pinned down ready for dissection.

Jools stared back.

'I think this will be no problem,' he decided at last. 'I have an attic.'

She tried to fix his accent: German? Dutch? No, further east.

He reached in his pocket and fished out a thick notebook, tore out part of a page and scribbled something on it before handing it to Chas. 'I give you my address,' he said. 'Come to me tomorrow. At six p.m., not before. Before that I am sleeping. I must go to work now.' He got up and, raising his battered trilby, gave Jools a little bow. 'Until tomorrow, Miss Julie. At six,' he reminded Chas. Off he toddled, leaving his port-and-lemon still untasted on the table.

They looked at the scrap of paper. It said:

Professor Arminius Hollander
34 Park Road.

'So what exactly is this job he's offering you?' asked Jools, plonking herself down beside Chas, where the old man had sat.

He gave a faint smile. 'Housekeeper. Seems he can't find a woman to come in and clean for longer than a week before they fall out. Someone suggested a bloke, living in, might suit him better.'

'You're kidding! What do you know about keeping house?'

'I can pick it up as I go along. It can't be difficult if women do it.'

She refused to rise to that one. 'Why do you want this job?'

'I'd like us to stay here for a bit. At least two years. So you can go to school.'

'I've been to school.' On and off. Even collected a handful of GCSEs, here and there, with Chas's help.

'You ought to get some A levels.'

'What for?'

'So you can go to university, if you want.'

'If I want? Or if you want? Are you trying to get rid of me? If you're tired of having me around, just say so and I'll go.'

'I want you to have the chance to live a more normal life, that's all.'

'Define normal. We're fine as we are, aren't we?'

'We can't go on drifting for ever.'

'Why not? Anyway, it's too late: term's started.'

'You can catch up. Easy. You've done it before.' He gave her a mischievous look. 'Are we going to have a fight about this?'

Picking a fight with Chas was like taking on Bugs Bunny: he never lost his temper, just sidestepped whatever you threw at him until you were exhausted. Then he'd take out the clarinet and start to play. It was never worth it.

'All right,' she said, 'I'll give it a go. I can always get myself excluded.'

He gave her a quick hug. 'That's my girl!'

Park Road ran all along one side of the park, no surprises there. Tall iron railings and a thicket of shrubs blocked off any view of it that might once have been enjoyed by the houses across the road. They stood aloof, like a row of stout Victorian matrons, trying hard to pretend they hadn't come down in the world and been turned into flats and solicitors' offices.

Number 34 was like a gawky spinster among them, too tall for its width. In an effort to look less conspicuous it had turned itself sideways and sunk up to its knees, turning the ground floor into a semi-basement. The front door was at the side, up a short flight of steps.

Professor Arminius Hollander had it open almost before they'd had time to knock and drew them into the hallway, which was unlit except for the coloured light filtering through the glass panes of the door.

'So!' he announced. 'We will begin at the beginning, yes? This way.'

Obediently they followed him down a steep flight of stairs, with an awkward right-angled turn, into the semi-basement. At the front was the kitchen, with a stone sink and an ancient kitchen-range. Years, it must be, since anyone had cooked on it. At the back was what was destined to be Chas's bedroom, with a tiny bathroom converted from the old larder. It was hard to think of anything polite to say, so they nodded and said nothing. Then the old man led them back up to the hall where they'd started, and his own two living-rooms leading off it. At the back was the dining-room, looking out over a tangled garden. Jools's growing impression was of a time capsule from the 1950s, as if the house had died then and been left unburied. Brown paint and linoleum and cold, stale air. As for the furniture—

'These things please me,' the Professor suddenly remarked, as if he'd read her mind. 'They are built to last – as I am. How old do you think I am?' He beamed, waiting for her answer, the dim light of the landing reflecting off his spectacles.

'I – er – ' It was one of those unanswerable questions.

'As old as my tongue and a little older than my teeth!' he cried triumphantly. A joke! An English joke, but Jools wasn't laughing. As he spoke, he'd opened the other door and she found herself staring into utter darkness, out of which dozens of eyes shone back, unblinking.

Then Chas felt for the light and switched it on and she saw the stuffed animals, foxes, badgers, rats, bats and owls, swinging from the ceiling, draped on chairs and occasional tables, crouched on the bookcases that lined the walls and on the pelmet above the dark velvet curtains that shut out the dying of the day.

'My study,' the Professor explained, 'is of the creatures of the night. These are my companions. My inspirations, yes?'

Poor things. It was a relief when he closed the door on them and led the way onward and upward, still talking, still explaining: 'My study, as I say, is of the creatures of the night and so I must keep the hours they do. This is no problem for you?'

Chas shook his head. 'No problem.' Musicians are night people too.

'Much of the day,' the old man continued, a little breathless now, from the stairs, 'I sleep, in here . . .' He showed them, briefly, the room at the back of the house, with its en suite bathroom.

'And this room?' asked Chas, indicating the door across the landing.

The old man paused. 'In this room is nothing of

17

interest. It is locked.' He patted his pocket. 'I myself will keep the key. Let us go on.'

On they went, up the last, narrower flight of stairs, to the two attics. They were both crammed with junk, but the one at the front had possibilities, Jools decided. The way the ceiling curved down almost to the floor reminded her of an upturned boat, like the Peggottys' house in *David Copperfield*. The view from the window was nothing but tossing treetops and the empty sky. You had to get right up close before you could see down into the street. Oh, yes, she could live here for two years: no problem.

There was even an old iron bedstead standing ready, with flaking purple paint (soon strip that off!) and one leg shorter than the rest and a mattress pounded solid over the years. She'd slept on worse.

'Well? What do you think?' The Professor stood with his hands folded across his unevenly buttoned cardigan, blinking through his glasses. He seemed pathetically anxious now that they should like the place and want to stay.

Chas looked at Jools and raised an eyebrow.

'It's OK,' she said.

★　　★　　★

They went straight back to Albie's and fetched their stuff. No point in waiting for Brenda to sling them out in the morning.

They moved in that night.

The following day Albie came round to give Chas a hand with shifting the heavy items out of the front attic into the back. First they had to restack the stuff that was in there already, but two into one will go, with a bit of argument and a lot of thumping and scraping and dropping things. Every now and then one of them would remember the Professor, who was supposed to be sleeping down below, and they'd shush one another and move about on tiptoe for a while. Then gradually the noise level would creep up to what it had been before.

There wasn't a sound from the back bedroom. The rest of the house stayed quiet as the grave.

Then Albie had to go, because he'd told Brenda he was just popping out to get the paint for the spare room and that was four hours ago. Chas went with him, to lend a hand, like he'd promised. Jools doubted whether even Chas could sweet-talk Brenda, so she stayed behind to carry on cleaning out her attic room, washing down the paintwork, scrubbing the floor.

In an old trunk, she found a length of yellow parachute silk, which she draped over the window in lieu of curtains, tying it back with scraps of jewellery and a heavy silver cross on a chain, a souvenir of Glastonbury. There were old shawls, too, of handworked embroidery and lace, to drape about with the aid of drawing-pins, and pillows – a bit musty – that she could wrap like parcels, for lounging on.

The floor of bare boards was a problem. She knew there was no one in the room below for her to disturb but it still bothered her, hearing her own footsteps as she moved about, so she kicked off her shoes and went barefoot.

Then she found a book of old wallpaper samples and started cutting them out and piecing them together, with some idea of covering the end wall in patchwork.

It grew dark without her noticing. The streetlamp opposite, of course, held back the night. At length, stiff and cold, she gathered up the last of the clutter and carried it down to the dustbin by the gate.

As she turned away, she saw him. A young man, standing in the lamplight, watching, waiting, staring up at the house, at the window of her room. Then, without seeming to turn, he was watching her watching him. He smiled. Before she could react, she heard a window suddenly pushed up and saw the Professor's silhouette, dark against the shadows of the room behind him – the room below hers.

When she looked back, the young man had gone. Not a movement, up and down the lamplit street.

From above her she heard the Professor's voice calling softly: 'Liesl! Liesl, my darling!'

Who – or what – was Liesl? A cat? There was the cat – there! Slinking along by the tall iron railings, moving from light to shadow and back again. A cat, with its own room, up on the second floor? Why not? And when it died, the Professor would probably have it stuffed and it would join the rest of his night-time companions.

'Liesl?'

The cat glanced disdainfully over its shoulder, then slid between the railings and was swallowed up by the darkness.

CHAPTER TWO

The following Monday, Jools started school. Time to put away adult things and become a child again, like having her feet forced into shoes she'd long ago grown out of. Having her day cut up for her into manageable bite-sized pieces, and being told how and where each piece was to be spent.

Every class thinks it's unique, but the main cast of characters is always pretty much the same.

She had no trouble picking out the Sporting Hero and the Computer Geek; the Oxbridge Hopeful and the Clown; the Bully and the Born Victim. There was the kid with spots that no one sits next to. He thinks it's the zits, but if he looked like Keanu Reeves he'd still be a social failure: it's in the genes. There was the Most Popular Girl, whom Jools immediately dubbed the Princess Caraboo after another con-artist who managed to convince the world at large that she was someone important. She was surrounded by her adoring fans, all dressed in pleated mini-skirts and V-necked sweaters. Some time in the distant past – about last Wednesday week – the Princess must have decreed that this outfit would be *de rigueur* for the coming term. Now they'd all nagged their mothers into buying it, she'd switched to a slinky, ankle-length number with a side-slit almost up to her knickers.

At the back of the room, Jools caught a glimpse of Joseph with a small group of friends. He gave her a quick, shy smile, winked and turned away.

Jools got the message. When asked if she already knew anyone there, she answered no.

So she found herself sitting next to a girl called Megan. Meg seemed OK, except she was so straight that she still let her mother choose the clothes she wore. High-necked navy sweater and plain grey skirt, very chic.

First lesson was Eng. Lit. *Othello*. The story so far: Iago has somehow managed to convince Othello that his new wife Desdemona is having an affair with his friend Cassio. As far as Jools could see, Othello's problem was simple: no sense of humour. He wouldn't recognise a wind-up if it walked up and poked him in the eye. This is not tragic: it is sad. But she kept this view to herself. Ms Eng. Lit. didn't seem the type to welcome radical new ideas.

On the other hand, the young guy fresh out of teacher training who took sociology practically begged them to participate – um, that is, if they'd got any suggestions – um, thoughts – especially if it was based on their actual experience . . .

There seemed to be a common agreement that they should let him sweat it out alone for the full fifty minutes. For his own good. If he couldn't cope with an A level group unaided, he'd be lucky if year nine let him live.

Jools had chosen French as her third subject. French ought to be a doddle, thanks to summers spent busking through the hill towns of south-west France. Chatting away to Mademoiselle, the school reek of chalk-dust, cheap polish and piss vanished in a roadside haze of thyme and broom; memories of window boxes spilling over with bright geraniums and short, broad men in berets walking impossibly small dogs. And warm, starlit evenings outside pavement cafés, with the music playing on and on . . .

Back home in England, however, the natives were getting restless. Fidgeting of the group round Princess Caraboo. Knowing glances exchanged by the rest of the class. It wasn't until after school that Meg explained why. 'It's Tanith—'

'Princess Caraboo?'

Meg gave a slow smile. 'Yes! Oh, what a gorgeous name! Did you make it up?'

'No,' said Jools. 'What about her?'

'Well, it's just that her people have got this place in the Dordogne, where they go every summer, so when it comes to speaking French . . .'

'I just upstaged the star of the show. Great!' Jools lifted up her head and gave a wolf-like howl. 'One day down, how many to go? Will I ever survive?'

'The first day's bound to be the worst,' said Meg sensibly. She hesitated. 'My mother doesn't get in until six. We could walk into town together. Look round the shops. Have a coffee. If you like.'

'I like! Come on.'

Jools was used to finding her way round new places. She'd already worked out pretty well how this one was put together. She headed straight for the underpass, so as to cross the main road.

'Not that way,' Meg called sharply.

Jools frowned. 'Why not?' She could see the shops just the other side.

'That's Rats' Alley. We never go that way.'

'Oh, let's!' Rats' Alley. The name conjured up echoes in her memory: something she'd read. A place where people came to die. One thing they'd never gone short of was books. Chas used to buy them from second-hand stalls. Once read, he'd sell them on, often at a profit.

'Have people actually died down there?' Jools demanded. 'How many? How many dead men?' she called, as she chased after Meg down a sidestreet.'

'I don't know.' Across the street they went and back again to the place opposite where they'd started.

'Dozens? Hundreds?'

Meg stopped briefly and turned to face her. 'Look. The place has just got a bad reputation, that's all. It doesn't take much longer to walk round.'

Along they went again and across a footbridge.

'What kind of bad reputation?' Jools wanted to know. 'Have people died down there?'

'Some. I suppose. Over the years. Everyone's got to die somewhere.'

As they moved away down the street, crossed at the traffic-lights, then came back again on the other side, Jools tried to keep count of the people who did use the underpass. A lot of them had a pinched, hunted look about them, but that probably had more to do with the fact that they seemed to be headed towards the grim tower blocks in the near distance. Living in those places was enough to make anyone tired of life.

The two of them mooched around the shops for a while, trying on hats, leafing through magazines, picking out CDs and putting them back, not buying anything except a couple of Cokes that Meg paid for.

Then, in the tiny shopping arcade, as all the shops were closing, they came upon the Princess Caraboo and her entourage, draped round the ornamental fountain like ungainly giggling nymphs.

The reason for their girlish excitement stood lounging against a pillar, hands in his pockets, just killing time until something, or someone, more amusing came along. Jools recognised the young man she'd last seen standing in the lamplight opposite her window. She was aware of him watching her again now, as Tanith stirred herself sufficiently to block their path.

Megan, too ladylike to swear, groaned under her breath.

'Jools!' said Tanith.

'Tanith!' Jools answered. Pistols at dawn wouldn't have been out of order. But an olive branch was what was called for, if she didn't want the whole gang bugging her for the next two years. Not something she was good at. She forced herself to offer a sprig: 'Speaking French,' she shrugged, 'it's nothing special. Millions of French kids manage it before they ever learn a word of English.'

Tanith considered this point.

Out of the corner of her eye, Jools could see he was still watching. Watching her, not Tanith.

'Jools,' said Tanith again, pensively this time.

29

'That's me,' she answered cheerfully.

'What's it short for? Julie? Juliet? Julian?' Tanith smirked, with a camp little toss of her head.

Chas had registered her name as Julie after her mother, but he could never bring himself to say it, so she'd been Jools ever since she could remember. This was not something she felt ready to share with Princess Caraboo.

'Just call me Jools,' she said.

'Jools!' he repeated softly. The first time she'd heard his voice. Or was it the first time? She felt a shiver run down her spine, as if someone had just walked over her grave. 'Glad you could make it,' the young man said, as he moved towards her.

Tanith, suddenly uncertain, asked, 'Do you two know each other?'

'Oh, yes,' he said lazily. 'We go way back. Don't we, Jools?' His eyes were blue-green, like the sea, and sparkling, full of mischief, daring her to contradict him.

Abruptly Tanith changed gear, into let's-be-friends. 'Nice jacket.' She meant it. 'Where can I get one like it?' she demanded, feeling the fabric between finger and thumb.

'You can't,' said Jools. 'It was made specially for me.'

'Who by?'

By Lady Rachel, of No Fixed Abode, who tells fortunes for a living and talks to her dead baby, Sam. A fine boy he's grown into, since he passed over into the spirit world. If he likes you, he'll tell Lady Rachel how to design a coat just for you, with embroidery and appliqué, and beads, and bits of shi-sha glass.

'A friend,' said Jools.

'Will you give me her address?'

'She hasn't got one.'

'I'll buy yours, then. Give you twice what you paid.'

Twice nothing is nothing.

'It's not for sale.'

Stand-off.

Still those sea-green eyes were watching her, willing her to remember . . .

All she could think to do was play for time. She pulled Meg forward. 'Do you know Meg? Meg, this is—'

There was a fraction of a pause – deliberate? – before

he picked up his cue: 'Nick Fleming. You can come with us.' Faintest stress there on the 'you', leaving the rest of them out in the cold. 'Time we were going! See you later, Tanith!' he called over his shoulder, already leading Meg with one hand and the other arm wrapped tight round Jools, racing them away, out of the arcade and across the street and through the iron gates of the park.

But who was he? Jools searched her memory as they dodged the traffic: if he knew her, she must know him. A traveller? No, too spruce. A musician? Possibly: but surely she would have remembered Nick Fleming, with his long, pale hands and face and the flame-red lights in his dark hair. Perhaps some kind of a magician. There were always guys around who'd taught themselves to juggle, tumble, or do simple conjuring tricks, as much for their own amusement as to keep the kids entertained.

By the pond, where the ducks were still swimming round the floodlit fountain, he suddenly stooped down and picked up a dark green pebble. He cupped it in his hands, caressing it, murmuring softly. When he opened his hand to show them, the pebble had become a small green frog. Jools knew for sure it was a frog because of the way it kicked its little legs when he threw it into the water. It landed with a faint splash. Then a duck caught it up in its beak and swallowed it whole.

Jools heard Meg give a faint cry of distress, but Nick, with a laugh, was already turning away.

He bumped into a man hurrying by. A little man, with a ginger toothbrush moustache and a pork-pie hat, who must have had a bad day because instead of muttering Sorry, and going on his way, he started giving Nick a mouthful about not looking where he was going, showing more consideration, etc., etc.

Nick only smiled at him. 'What does he remind you of, Jools? A little dog? Let's turn him into a dog!' Softly he growled in his throat, still staring at the man. 'Grrr-ap!' Growling over again, until—

'Grrapp!' the man snapped back. He went on barking. 'Yap, yap, yap!' The man was barking like a dog, such an earnest look on his face. 'Yap, yap, yap!' They walked away, leaving him still barking, people gathering round, staring, laughing. Jools was entranced, hardly aware of Meg trying to pull away, already confused by this strange friend of hers.

On they went, until they stood on the highest point of the park, looking down at the rest of the world scurrying home, like so many busy insects.

'Let's run!' said Nick. He seized their hands and they set off down the hill, gathering speed, until Jools couldn't feel her feet touch the ground. Faster and faster they went, past office workers weighed down with supermarket bags and mothers dragging little kids and sleepy babies in push-chairs, all in a separate, slow-motion world. The three of them moved so fast they seemed invisible, except to an old wino, who stood staring after them with a bottle of cheap sherry poised halfway to his mouth.

Gradually their pace slowed and they came to a halt by the gate leading out into Park Road.

'Time you were going, Meg,' Nick said. He wasn't even out of breath. 'It's gone six. Your mother will be worried.'

'Yes.' Meg nodded. 'I really should go. You'll be all right, Jools?'

'I'll be fine,' said Jools.

'See you tomorrow, then.' Meg turned and walked quickly away.

'She doesn't like me,' murmured Nick. 'I wonder why? Not that it matters. I don't like her either. I think if I were to take a bite out of her, she'd taste of buttermilk and lettuce.'

Jools grinned. 'And what would I taste of?'

'You, Little Red Riding Hood?' He thought for a moment. 'You would taste exactly like your mother.'

'My mother's dead.'

'I know.' His sadness was immediate and personal and real. How old was he? Eighteen? Surely no more than twenty. He couldn't have known her mother – not so as to remember.

'What do you know about my mother?'

He hesitated. 'What has Chas told you?'

'Nothing. Nothing at all.'

'Then you must ask him,' he said wisely.

Sea-green eyes stared into hers, stirring a memory from so far back – 'I know I should remember you,' Jools confessed at last. 'But I don't. Who are you? Where do you come from?'

He spread his arms wide: 'Everywhere. Nowhere. Like you. We are two of a kind, you and I, Jools.' He frowned and shook his head. 'No! I can't go on calling you that. I shall call you Juliette – little Julie. Now I must go.'

'When will I see you again?'

'Soon. I promise.' She felt his cold lips brush her cheek. 'I won't be far away.' Then he was lost in the shadows.

As Jools moved towards the house, a voice above her said, 'Miss Julie?'

She jumped half out of her skin. The Prof was standing at the top of the front steps. How long had he been watching there?

'Who was that with you?' he asked.

'No one. Just a friend.'

'A school-friend?'

'That's right,' she agreed, escaping past him into the house. She didn't feel bad about lying to him. It was none of his business.

She watched him shuffle off down the road, apparently satisfied. Behind him, the cat emerged from the shadows and stalked silently along in his wake, its tail erect and swaying in time to the gait of his short legs.

The smell of garlic hit her before she'd closed the door. Downstairs, in the kitchen, she found Chas busy at the stove.

'It's a recipe of the Professor's,' he explained. 'He particularly wanted you to try it.'

'Didn't you tell him I hate garlic?' The first time she'd had it, nobody had warned her. She had thought the meat was off, but politely ate it anyway, firmly expecting to be dead of food poisoning by morning. Garlic had left her feeling queasy ever since. She hung her coat on the door and dumped her school-bag on the carefully laid table.

'Tell me about my mother,' she said.

'What, now?' He reached for the pepper-mill.

'Why not now?'

'You've never asked before.' He was grinding pepper into the saucepan – too much pepper, whatever else he'd got in there.

'I'm asking now. Am I like her?'

He glanced at her, frowning slightly, then turned

away, concentrating his attention on the stinking mess on the stove. 'No,' he said. 'You're nothing like her.'

Jools let that sink in. Then, 'Think I'll be a veggie for this evening,' she said. 'Homework.' She helped herself to bread, cheese and fruit and took it up to her room to eat.

Later she heard the sad, sweet song of the clarinet creeping up the stairs to find her. 'Jailhouse Blues'. She knew the words by heart. He was telling her he was lonely and wanted to talk, but she didn't go down again.

CHAPTER THREE

They'd never seemed so far apart before, not even on her first day at infants' school. As he'd left her then, he'd given her a tiny pink plastic elephant out of a Christmas cracker to hold on tight to. 'Squeeze it hard and think of me and I'll be thinking of you,' he promised. But the elephant had gone AWOL long ago and the cold, dead air of 34 Park Road hung heavy between them, the study with its creatures stranded somewhere between life and death and in the room between – what?

Sometimes after dark she heard the Professor shuffling about in there, opening the window, the name 'Liesl!' repeated over and over again. Once she woke up in the middle of the night and thought she heard the sound of someone crying. But every time she tried the door, she found it locked and there was a sense of total emptiness.

Outside, the world was dying. Trees dressed themselves in a last defiant blaze of yellow and red before the wind whipped the leaves from the branches and carried them off in a whirling dance of death, then suddenly lost interest, leaving them to fester and rot in slithery heaps.

I'm getting old, thought Jools mournfully. I'm sinking into middle age and I haven't finished being young! Any other time, Chas would have noticed her mood and done something totally wild and unexpected to lift her out of it, but Chas, when he was home, was busy learning how to keep house, coping with the vagaries of the kitchen stove, which seemed to have a mind of its own and an insatiable appetite for coal. She watched the coalman delivering one day, pouring it down a chute from outside straight into the cupboard in the basement passage. Neat.

Chas talked to the Professor. She didn't.

'What does the Prof do, exactly?' Jools asked him.

Chas said, 'He writes. He studies. He wanders

the streets, looking for inspiration. He calls himself a psychic investigator. Ghosts, poltergeists, flying saucers or fairies at the bottom of the garden, he's the man you send for when all else fails.'

'He makes a living out of it? Kushti! We could do that!'

'Not if you want to keep your sanity.'

'But he's the good guy?'

'That's right.'

'He still gives me the creeps.'

Jools kept to her room while the Professor was shuffling about the house. By the time he went out, Chas was usually on his way too, down to the pub to work or for another run-through with the band. And where was Nick Fleming when she needed him? Not that she did need him, not specially. It was just odd, remembering his last words to her, that she hadn't seen him around again, not in the shopping area, or in the park, though every day she walked to the top of the little hill and looked all around.

On the second Thursday afternoon she bunked off school. Double sociology. She could read it up in about twenty minutes. She was doing the poor young guy a favour, really, one less blank face staring at him.

She walked to the highest point of the park and stood with her eyes closed and her arms spread wide, trying to remember how it had felt to fly . . .

Then she heard the sound of music. A concertina.

By the main gate, opposite the shopping arcade, she found Joseph, in his top hat and his coat of many colours. With one foot he worked the wooden doll hung with tiny bells, so that it danced in time to the music. Folk music, lifting her spirits, reminding her feet of an Irish jig taught to her once by an old tinker-woman. All round the town she'd danced, with the tinker-woman playing on a hurdy-gurdy, had come back with a pocketful of money and found Chas close to tears because he thought he'd lost her. He'd had the whole camp out searching the woods and fields.

'Thirsty work, Joseph?' she heard herself say, when he finally stopped playing.

He nodded and smiled.

She crossed the road to the newsagent's and came back with two cans of shandy, non-alcoholic. They sat side by side on the low wall just inside the gate.

'Free period?' asked Joseph.

She shook her head. 'You?'

'Double human biology. Don't tell my mum. We need the money.'

They sat in companionable silence for a while.

'You coming tonight?' asked Joseph.

'Coming where?'

'Down the Spotted Cow. Jazz night. Chas must have told you.'

'Oh. Yeah.' He hadn't. 'He said he got the piano fixed.'

'Yep.'

'I thought you'd be more pleased.'

'I would, if the guys'd let me play. They said I should stick to the drums for the time being.'

'That's not fair.'

'I'm not going to make waves. I don't mind playing drums. It's just, like, in my soul, I feel I'm a piano-man. You know what I mean?'

Jools nodded.

'Anyway, Albie said he'd try and find someone to dep for me. You play at all?'

'Drums?'

'Anything.'

She shook her head. 'Women can't play jazz.'

He stared at her, incredulous. 'That was yesterday, man! The day before that they were saying white men couldn't play. Maybe you sing a bit?'

'I don't sing.' She took a swig of shandy. 'My mother was a singer. She died.'

'That's tough.'

'I wouldn't know. I was just a few days old.'

Silence.

'Where do you live?' she asked.

He pointed towards the tower blocks (no getting away from them, even here). 'Across the main road. Through the underpass.'

'Rats' Alley.'

'Yeah. You heard about Rats' Alley?' He grinned. 'My nan used to tell us: "You better be good. Else that old loogaroo, he'll come creeping out of Rats' Alley and he'll suck out your soul and you'll go limping through the world, yes, you will, without a soul to call your own."'

'That wasn't what I heard. I got the impression it's the sort of place where people go to die.'

'Maybe. Maybe Rats' Alley's one of those places that make you feel like giving up on life. Maybe it's the kind of place that draws you to it when you're feeling down. Try walking through there some night after dark. I'll swear there's something in the air that makes you wonder if it's worth putting in the effort to climb back out again. That's that old loogaroo, climbing on your back, trying to suck out your soul.'

'Spooky!' said Jools. 'I must try it.'

Laughing, he aimed his empty can at the litter bin, threw it and missed. Jools scooped it up and tossed it in with hers.

'See you later, then,' said Joseph. 'You gotta hear Josie sing! Besides, I owe you a drink, right?'

Jools nodded. 'See you later.'

Jazz can't be hurried: it has to be allowed to happen in its own good time. Most of the punters knew this and were still gathered in the bar of the Spotted Cow at nine o'clock, although the music had been scheduled to start at half past eight. Ninja, who played trumpet, hadn't even arrived yet. Dave – guitar and banjo – was still in the bar with a bunch of his mates from the barracks. Chas, Albie and Joseph had set up their gear ready in the back room. The drum kit took up most of the tiny stage. Once Joseph was squeezed in behind it, he had to stay there until the others let him out.

The room itself, in contrast to the bar, was a lot bigger than it looked. Jools hadn't noticed the mezzanine before. Chairs and tables were set out on both levels and candles in wax-encrusted bottles. One or two punters sitting about. Murmur of conversation. Then Ninja finally arrived. 'Sorry, fellas. Traffic on the motorway. Van in front of me with a duff exhaust. If I'd known how long we were going to be sitting there, I'd've got out and fixed it for him. My mouth's so dry now I couldn't spit a sixpence, never mind play. Someone fetch me a pint, quick!'

'I'll go,' offered Jools.

'You're an angel! Lager, in a mug.'

Drinks for the band were on the house. Jools slid behind the bar and drew off the lager herself. No hurrying it. Time to look around, not expecting to see anyone she knew. And there he was. Nick Fleming. No mistaking that pale face. For a moment his eyes seemed to meet hers, but he gave no sign of recognising her. Must be his reflection, a trick of the mirrors, which meant he was sitting somewhere over to her left. Where was he? He must be there somewhere.

Lager was running over her hand. She turned off the tap, wiped the glass and carried it into the back room.

As she was handing it to Ninja, Albie stopped murmuring sweet nothings to Samantha to remark, 'Talking of finding someone to do a spot of depping for you on the drums, Joseph, it so happens I had a call from an old mate of ours the other day. Someone Chas'll remember.'

Chas set down his glass on the table beside him. 'A drummer, you say? That narrows it down to double figures.'

Albie smiled, snuggling up to Samantha again. 'Not just any drummer. This guy really could play the devil's music.' An angry little *rat-a-tat-tat!* came from the snare-drum. 'No disrespect, Joseph.'

A clash of cymbals signalled, Apology accepted.

Albie began to pluck at Samantha's strings. 'Cast

47

your mind back, Chas,' he urged, 'ten, twelve years. You must remember! He remembers you. Asked me to mention his name. Think, Chas!'

Chas *was* thinking; thinking so hard, he might have been turned to stone.

'Nick!' Albie burst out at last. 'Nick Fleming!'

Nick Fleming? Jools frowned: twelve, or even ten years ago, the Nick Fleming she'd met would have been just a little kid.

'Twelve years, eh?' mused Albie. 'Must be.'

'Sixteen,' Chas said softly. 'It was sixteen years ago.'

Albie stared at him. Glanced at Jools. His lips formed the words, 'Oh, sh—!' He turned away and went through the motions of banging his head against the wall.

Chas closed his eyes, lifted the clarinet to his lips and began to play, very softly and, oh, so sweetly, 'Hushabye', notes falling like tears into the surrounding silence. It almost broke your heart to hear him.

After a while, Joseph joined in, but quietly, a steady, shuffling rhythm on the drums. Then Albie:

Sorry, mate. My big mouth! Ninja sat quietly, sipping his pint, until Chas had played the sadness out of him. Not until the last notes died away, did Ninja put down his glass. He carefully wiped his mouth, picked up the trumpet and launched straight into 'King Kong', taking it nice and loose, not too fast. A few bars in, Chas came in with the counter-melody, fingers dancing over the keys, as though he hadn't a care in the world.

Jools moved against the sudden tide of customers flowing in from the bar: she had to talk to Nick. Now she could see him! He was sitting at a table in the far corner, with a fluffy blonde girl – candy-floss hair and quite a thirst on her. Her glass was empty, while his was still full. As Jools watched, the two glasses seemed to change places and the blonde drained the second one.

Something in his manner told her he knew she was watching, but he didn't so much as glance her way, only bent his head close to the girl's and whispered something in her ear. She smiled and nodded and they both got up to go. *So that's how you want to play it, Nick Fleming, is it? See if I care.*

She watched them weaving their way through the

still-crowded bar. The general shift towards the back had just given the rest more elbow-room. As the couple reached the door, it opened and Professor Hollander came in. He glanced around the bar in some surprise – not much chance of a quiet port-and-lemon tonight – then followed Nick and the girl out again into the darkness.

In the back room, Josie had begun to sing. 'Frankie and Johnny'. Jools moved closer to listen. Joseph was right; it was worth coming tonight, just to hear Josie sing. White woman; black voice. Sensational.

Candles glowed, casting strange shadows, reflecting off glasses. Even the smoke hung in the air, listening. Too much smoke to be healthy, but who wants to live for ever? Jazz is now. Catch each note, enjoy it and then let it die. You'll never hear it quite this way again and that's the beauty of it. A recording's no more like the real thing than the stuffed dead creatures in the Professor's study.

The applause was like people waking out of a dream.

Then, without warning, Josie changed the mood. A glance at Ninja, who nodded and played a few notes by way of introduction, then she started belting out 'I wish I could shimmy like my sister Kate' with all the actions.

Kate, reflected Jools, must register round about nine on the Richter scale.

The next evening, Jools was sitting alone in her eyrie when she heard slow footsteps coming up the stairs.

Chas? No, today was Friday. Chas was working down at the Spotted Cow. Besides, Chas's footsteps were lighter, quicker. It must be the Professor. What did he want? Shuffling, hesitant, the steps came nearer and stopped outside. She could hear him breathing heavily, trying to get his breath back.

He knocked.

Perhaps if she sat very quiet and still he'd think she'd gone out too and go away.

He knocked again, harder, more insistent.

With a sigh, she untangled her feet from the sleeping bag that she'd been using to keep warm and went to open the door.

'Miss Julie?' Eyes blinking in the sudden flood of light from the room. 'May I come in, please?'

Jools shrugged. 'It's your house.'

'I will consider that an invitation.' In he stepped, looking about him, nodding at the cushions, the bookshelves (two piles of bricks with planks between) and the patchwork wall (still incomplete and likely to stay that way). 'This is very nice,' he decided. 'Very good.'

He crossed over to the window, taking in the curtain drapery, the jewellery, the heavy silver cross. 'This, too, is good.' He tried the window catch and seemed pleased to find it stuck fast under countless generations of paint. 'Good, good.' He turned to face her. 'I do not want to frighten you, Miss Julie – your father says I must not frighten you—'

'I'm not frightened.'

'No? That does not mean there is no danger.'

'What danger?' she asked, since he seemed to be expecting her to say something.

'Out there. In the darkness.' He stared first at her, then down at his feet, then back at her again. 'How to explain? How to explain without you thinking I am just a crazy old man?' He steepled his fingers. 'We live in an age of science, Miss Julie. Is this not so? What science cannot explain is pie in the sky.

52

I also, though I come from a country where such things are readily believed, I was a man of science. I would have said such things cannot be – until I lost my wife. My Liesl.'

'Your wife?' Jools exclaimed. 'Liesl was your wife's name?'

He nodded. 'My Liesl. So young. So beautiful.' He took off his glasses and began to polish them vigorously. Without them, his face was strangely childlike, and vulnerable. 'I failed her,' he said sadly. 'But, be assured,' he placed his glasses back on his nose and looked her fearlessly in the eye, 'I will not make the same mistake again. Since then, I have made a study of these things. I know now what must be done! I will protect you, if I can. If not . . . We will not consider that possibility. By daylight, my dear, you are quite safe. By day, he sleeps. Here, in this room, also, you are secure. You have made this place your own. No one can enter without you inviting them. Outside, in the darkness – I think you will laugh if I tell you – garlic is some protection.'

'I hate garlic.'

'If you will not eat the garlic, will you humour this

crazy old man and carry some always in your pocket? It can do no harm. Here. I have something for you.' He fumbled in his pocket and drew out a small box. Inside was a silver crucifix on a chain. 'For you,' he said again. 'Promise me that you will always wear it. Put it on now. Let me see.'

Jools did as he asked. Why not, if it kept him happy? She was beginning to get the picture now. Garlic and crucifixes? Just to be sure, as he was leaving, she asked him straight out: 'What is it I'm supposed to be afraid of?'

'Why, the vampire, Miss Julie, the vampire! Goodnight.'

'Goodnight,' she said. 'Sweet dreams.'

She smiled to herself as she shut the door behind him, leaving him to grope his way downstairs in the dark.

CHAPTER FOUR

They didn't find the girl's body until late on the Sunday afternoon.

By Monday morning the whole park had been cordoned off while the police carried out an inch-by-inch ground search for clues.

The newspaper reports were sketchy – *A savage attack! A brutal murder!* Isn't all murder brutal and savage? – but the school bush-telegraph was fully operational: stabbed, over and over again!

'With a knife!' Well, of course with a knife: what else would it have been?

Stabbed over and over. He must have been a madman. Stabbing and slashing, until the knife finally pierced her heart. There was some disagreement as to whether the murderer had then hacked off her head, or whether it was the dog, in its excitement

at finding a new plaything, that had finished the job
for him.

'Ooh!'

'Eeek!'

The very idea brought squeals of horror from the
Princess's followers.

A dog out walking with its master.

'Just imagine!' the boys speculated. 'The dog
runs off—'

'Chasing a stick or something, and comes back with
the head in its jaws!'

'Carrying it by the hair! Yurgh!'

More screams from the fan club; hands over their
eyes, their mouths, their ears, like the three wise
monkeys.

Since Thursday night she'd lain there, gnawed at
already by rats and cats and urban foxes. 'Yurgh!'
again and double 'yurgh!' and one or two of them
near to tears and 'Will there be stress-counselling for
us, miss?'

'I mean, some of us almost *knew* her, miss – *I* knew
where she lived, anyway.'

Jools sat in silence, staring at the picture on the front

page of the newspaper that someone had brought in: a pretty, rather vacant face and blonde, candy-floss hair. There was no doubt in her mind that it was the same girl she'd seen in the pub with Nick Fleming. The police, it said, wanted to speak to a young man seen with her on the Thursday evening. In order to eliminate him from their inquiries. Of course: what other reason could they have?

She stayed late at school that evening, working on in the library until it was getting dark. In the dark she always felt safe, her senses sharpened; sounds, sights and smells all clearer than when they were muddled by daylight.

The quick way home across the park was still cut off by police cordons so she turned the other way, hurrying along till she reached the entrance to Rats' Alley. Stupid to be scared: the girl hadn't died down there, had she? She was killed up here, right out in the open.

Jools plunged down the steps. There should have been lights, but most of the bulbs were broken. And the tunnel curved, quite unnecessarily, making it gloomier still. There was no one else down there, just the echo of her own footsteps behind her. Even graffiti artists seemed to give the place a wide berth. Scraps of litter hitched a lift out on the first passing breeze so they could lower the tone of some place that hadn't already reached rock bottom.

Slowly she began to get the feeling that the other footsteps she could hear weren't just the echo of her own. A sense that there was someone very close behind. She turned abruptly. No one.

Silence. Traffic sounds, far, far above. And the drip, drip, drip of water. Smell of cold, dead air. Soon be out of here. She turned to go on her way.

Suddenly, he was between her and the light. Nick Fleming, casually standing a few metres in front of her.

'How did you do that?' she demanded.

'Do what?' he asked, all innocence.

'A moment ago you were behind me.'

'Oh, that! Just practice.'

Her heart was thumping so hard, she was surprised she couldn't hear it echoing off the walls. 'Well, don't do it again, OK?'

'I'm sorry,' he said gently. 'Please, don't be frightened.'

She realised, as she made to walk on, past him, that she wasn't frightened any more: just annoyed. 'A girl's been murdered, for heaven's sake!'

'Well, don't look at me!' he said amiably, falling into step beside her. 'I didn't do it.'

'You were with her on Thursday night. The police want to talk to you.'

'I know. But do I want to talk to them? I don't think so.'

At the place where the underground paths met, they came out into an open space where some optimistic town planner had put wooden benches round a raised bed of dusty shrubs that fought for air among the traffic fumes.

'It's you I want to talk to,' he said.

Suddenly he sat on one of the benches and pulled her down to sit beside him. He fingered the silver cross round her neck. 'That's pretty.'

'Professor Hollander gave it to me,' Jools told him, drawing away a little. 'Our landlord, you know?'

He nodded. 'I know him.'

'He said it would protect me.'

'Against what?'

'Vampires, I think,' she said, with a grin.

His face broke into a smile. 'What other precautions did he tell you to take? Eat up your garlic, dab a few drops of holy water behind your ears? Always carry a mirror with you, so you can check out any suspicious character, because it's a well-known fact that a vampire has no reflection? He'll be pinching communion wafers from the church next and crumbling them round doorways, like that evil old man in *Dracula*! Feeding that poor girl on the blood of living men! Of course she became a vampire. The old fool! What does he know?'

'What is there to know?'

'About vampires? I have some theories of my own. Perhaps we should think of them as creatures more to be pitied then feared? Would you like me to tell you about a family of vampires I once knew?'

'A family? Mummy Vampire, Daddy Vampire and Baby Vampire? I think I'm a bit old for that.'

'Juliette! This is not the Three Bears. This is a true story.'

In spite of herself, Jools shivered.

'Are you cold?' he asked her.

'A bit.'

'Soon have you warm.' He slipped his arm round her and she drew her feet up onto the bench, tucking them under her skirt. It was like being a little kid again, dozing by the campfire, being told a bedtime story.

'Let's see,' Nick began. 'Long ago and far away . . .'

'How far away?' asked Jools, sixteen-years-old-going-on-six.

'Somewhere in France.'

'France isn't far.'

'It was, in those days. As much as two weeks' ride from here, even in good weather.'

'What days? How long ago?'

'Five – no, nearer six hundred years now. Do you want to hear this story?'

'Of course I do.'

'Then be quiet and let me tell it.'

'OK. I'll be quiet.'

'OK. Six hundred years ago, then.' He gave a deep sigh. 'How time flies! If only we had more of it! A little more time, isn't that what we all want? There are scientists in California now who say there is no reason why we shouldn't live for two – even four hundred years.

'Six hundred years ago, in France, Flamel – that was our man's name; we should, perhaps, call him Maître Flamel, or Monsieur le Docteur, for he was a scholar, a philosopher, an alchemist – he *knew* it was possible for people to live much longer than they did, because the Bible told him so. In the old times, so the Good Book said, men like Methuselah and Adam and Noah had lived for nine hundred years and more. So he set out to rediscover the secret which would give him something very close to immortality. Together with his wife, Pernelle, he worked, researched, experimented, for three times seven years and three times seven again . . .

'At the end of all that time, what had he achieved? Nothing! Not so much as the means to extend his life by one more day – one hour – one minute! What was worse, he'd wasted the only life he had. And then one night as he sat in his garden, learning at last to love the world he would have to leave so soon – he hardly slept these days: each minute he had left was too precious to waste in sleep, yet he must have dozed a little, for when he opened his eyes a woman stood before him, tall, beautiful and wise. She was a vampire. A vampire, who'd fed on him while he slept. In drinking his blood, she'd learned to know his memories, his thoughts, his hopes, his dreams, as if they were her own. Now she offered to grant his dearest wish: life eternal!

'Flamel smiled and shook his head: what good was that to him now? Who'd want life eternal, old as he was, wrinkled, arthritic?

'She smiled, too; and she explained that to be a vampire is to slough off all outward signs of mortality, as a snake sheds its outworn skin.

'*Then* he was tempted: to be immortal *and* to be young again, so that he could do all those things he'd never had time for! There was still so much to see! So much to learn! There was a price to pay, of course.' He paused. 'The usual price for a bargain made with the Devil. His immortal soul. After all, as she pointed out, he'd have no further use for it if he was going to live in this world for ever . . . What would you have done, Juliette?'

Jools thought for a bit. 'I'd have wanted to read the small print. The Devil's not going to buy remaindered goods, right? There's got to be a catch.'

'Flamel couldn't see one – and he was a clever man. It's now or never! Your one and only chance of immortality! What will you do?'

'He went for it, right? Or else there'd be no story.'

He smiled. 'As you say: he went for it. She opened the vein at her wrist and gave him her blood to suck. As he drank the blood of the vampire, he felt the weight of fifty years slipping away. He felt younger – fitter – stronger than he could ever remember being in his whole life before. He saw the world for the first time clearly, through a vampire's eyes: the colours and the textures! He realised he could hear each tiny sound in the air around him: the squeak of a bat, the beat of a moth's wing caught in a spider's web. He could distinguish the scent of every flower in the night air, individually! He never saw the woman go, just sat there, spellbound, until the sun came up.

'This much is true: a vampire cannot bear direct sunlight, there's some change in the pigment of the skin, so that it blisters if the sun so much as touches it. But what does he want with garish sunlight, when he can see so clearly by night? If you could only see the stars as a vampire sees them! Not just points of light, but tiny, jewel-bright pools of colour, red and blue and orange and green.

'Then he went upstairs to find Pernelle. You remember his wife, Pernelle?

'Poor Pernelle! She'd given her whole life to helping him with his work. Now he asked her to give up her immortal soul, so they could share eternity together. Out of love for him, she gave it. Gave up her soul and drank his blood and became a vampire in her turn, so she could share his exile. She knew he'd never manage on his own.

'They had to leave the friends they knew. They never dared stay in one place too long, in case people noticed that they never ate or drank; never went out in daylight; never grew older. Witches were burned, in those days. A vampire can't be killed by fire, but he can still burn, still feel the pain.' His voice faltered for a moment, then he recovered himself. 'Better not to risk it, keep moving on.

'Flamel studied arts, science, medicine, languages,

music . . . They even joined a travelling circus for a while, so that he could learn conjuring, juggling, rope-dancing – why not, since he had all the time in the world?

'The blood-drinking came later. There's a reason for that. A vampire is already immortal; he doesn't need blood to stay alive or to remain young. Only to remember what it feels like to be human again, to feel a part of the times he's living through. Without the blood, he would very soon become a monster. Try to understand this, Juliette. They'd been born at the end of the Middle Ages, when men believed that the earth was flat; that this world was the centre of the universe; the world was made for man and man was made in the image of God. Then suddenly it's the Renaissance: new arts, new sciences, new inventions, new ideas! The new craft of printing, spreading these ideas amongst men who'd never even met each other! Wars between Christian and Christian, each army claiming that God was on their side. A whole new world discovered on the far side of the Atlantic. Flamel and Pernelle, as old people do, longed for a time when they were young and the world was a simpler place and kinder. But they weren't seventy years old; they were nearer two hundred.

'In the blood is the life. To drink blood from a living body is to share that life. Its memories, thoughts, hopes, fears. If you share a life, the last thing you want to do is end it – unless it's not worth living. They only took life from the fatally wounded, from the terminally ill, from those who lived in utter despair.

'Flamel was still happy as a child in a toyshop – every few years some new craze! But Pernelle longed for an end to it all.

'One night she kneeled beside a boy so badly wounded there was no hope, none at all . . . The battle had lasted barely an hour and now his life was over. His pain was worse than anything you can imagine, but his will to live was so strong that as the enemy moved across the battlefield, shooting or bayoneting anything that moved or groaned, he kept so still and silent that they passed him by. Yet Pernelle smelled him out. She saw his case was hopeless. All she could offer him was an easy death. But with the first taste of his blood, she knew that this one was different from the rest. There always came a moment when they were resigned to death. A feeling of – how shall I describe it? – total peace? joy? love? She envied them that. Perhaps that's what heaven is,' he said softly, 'that single moment of peace, suspended in eternity. But this one, she knew, would not resign himself: this one would give his soul for one more day!

'So, instead of sucking out his life's blood, she gave him life. She opened her vein and she let him drink.

'In 1761, Flamel and Pernelle attended the Paris opera, accompanied by their nineteen-year-old son.

'For a while, Pernelle was happy again, teaching her fledgeling vampire how to spread his wings; there was so much to show him, to share with him!

'Before she knew it, another thirty years had flown by. We're in Paris. The Revolution! The Terror. The guillotine.

'That's the one sure way to kill a vampire – to separate the head from the body. A stake through the heart, hammered straight through, with one blow – maybe, but it's difficult in practice. Pernelle knew that she'd never have a better chance of ending it all.

'It was easy to get yourself arrested in Paris

during the Revolution. Arrested, condemned and executed . . .

'The first the two men heard was a story circulating the Paris bars one evening of a woman guillotined that day, whose face, when she stepped from the tumbril, was so burned and blistered by the sun that the executioner and his assistant both refused to touch her, for fear of catching some terrible disease. She could have walked away unharmed. Instead she stepped forward and lay down in the shadow of the guillotine, offering her neck to the knife, so calmly, that those who came after her took courage from it.

'Some complained that she spoilt the whole day's entertainment; others said she must be a saint and were paying the executioner for a lock of her hair. It cost Flamel a tidy sum, I can tell you, to be allowed to take away her body entire. There we lose sight of him for a white.'

'What about the son?' asked Jools.

Very quietly he went on: 'He was less than seventy years old. That's young for a vampire, but already he was quite out of touch with the times he was living in. He began to take victim after victim, indiscriminately and without mercy, draining them dry in an attempt to understand why this thing had happened. You might say he went mad. What else was there to do? The world was mad. A world that would kill a sweet creature like Pernelle in the name of freedom and the brotherhood of man had to be mad!'

'I don't understand. I thought you said she wanted to die.'

Suddenly he was on his feet, swinging round to face her. 'Oh, you're still very young, aren't you?' he said contemptuously. 'She had no right to die! She had no right to do that to him!'

A woman, dragging a shopping trolley, emerged from one of the tunnels, took one startled look at Nick and bolted back the way she'd come.

'I'm sorry,' said Jools. 'What happened next?'

Nick thrust his hands into his pockets. 'That's enough for today. Your friend up there on the footbridge will be getting cold.'

'My friend?' Jools squinted up at the bridge, dazzled by the tall streetlamps. Anyway, it was too far away to make out more than a dark shape.

'Megan,' he said. 'She's been up there watching us ever since we sat down together.'

'But you can't just leave the story there!'

'That's all it is — a story.' He shrugged. 'I don't know how I'm going to end it yet. Another time I'll tell you. I shouldn't have lost my temper. I was thinking about — someone else. Come on.'

Obediently she gathered up her things, her bag, untangling the strap from among the shrubs and thorns.

'You've pricked your finger, Juliette.'

A single drop of blood, a perfect ruby, balanced on the end of her finger. He put it to his lips and she felt the blood well up, drawn off quite painlessly, like when they tested it at the donor centre.

A flick of his tongue and there wasn't a mark left to show.

He smiled. 'An excellent vintage. But still a little young.'

Then he put his arm round her shoulders and they walked through the tunnel out into the real world again.

CHAPTER FIVE

Meg was there ahead of them, apparently absorbed by the display of cold remedies in a chemist's window.

'She's waiting for me to go,' murmured Nick.

'Let her wait.'

'No. I must go.' He grinned mischievously. 'That taste of blood! I suddenly feel ravenously hungry.'

It was only after he'd gone that Jools remembered there'd been all sorts of questions she'd wanted to ask him. But there'd be other times. She was sure of it.

She walked over and stood beside Megan, still peering into the chemist's shop window. 'If you've got a cold,' said Jools, 'you'd be better off at home than hanging about on bridges.'

'I haven't got a cold,' sniffed Meg. 'I just thought – none of us ought to be walking home alone. Certainly not if they're walking through Rats' Alley.'

'That girl wasn't killed down Rats' Alley. Anyway I wasn't alone. Why didn't you come and say hallo?'

Meg started to walk away. 'I didn't want to. Who is he anyway?'

'Why don't you like him?'

'Something about him – the way he looks at you, as if he's trying to get inside your head. What is it they say about a smell of brimstone?'

'I think he smells delicious!' Not true, she thought. There's an odd thing! He doesn't smell of anything – not soap, or aftershave, or sweat – close your eyes and it's almost as if he's not there at all. 'You're not scared of the park, then?' she remarked, following Meg through the main gate. The path to Park Road from the main shopping centre was open again, so it was the quickest way home.

Meg gave her an exasperated look: there were police everywhere, and dogs, and men in raincoats who were either reporters or detectives, enough of them to protect a head of state.

Jools turned her face up towards the sky, wondering if what Nick had said about the stars was true. Tiny pools of colour, red and orange and

green and blue. No stars tonight. It was starting to rain.

'Meg,' said Jools, 'do you believe you've got a
soul?'

Meg gave her a surprised look. 'Of course.'

'I mean, what difference do you think it would
make if you hadn't got one? Would you know?'

Meg stopped to reflect. 'I think,' she said carefully,
'that having a soul is what makes us different from
the animals. Without it, there'd be no right or wrong,
no good or bad. Nothing you did would have any
meaning, any point to it.'

'What about when you died?'

'There'd be nothing. Oblivion. As if you'd never
existed.'

'A lot of people believe that anyway.'

'Do they? Do they, really, in their heart of hearts,
without a shred of hope? How can they imagine
it? Not even blackness – just nothing, for ever
and ever. It's like trying to get your mind round
the idea of eternity – like, what's at the end
of space, or what was there before time began.
There's got to be something. It doesn't have to

be heaven and hell – there's reincarnation. Or . . .
or there's . . .'

'Ghosts,' suggested Jools. 'I know a ghost. That is,
I know someone who talks to one. Her baby was
born dead. He tells her things she couldn't possibly
know any other way. I suppose he must have had a
soul already,' she added thoughtfully.

Or perhaps they'd given him one when they
christened him, stopping at the first lay-by they
came to, with water in an old plastic washing-up
bowl, because, three months premature or not, the
idea of throwing him away like unwanted baggage
was just too terrible. He had to have a name. Lorries
and holiday caravans thundering by, and people staring
out of the windows at the little group of travellers.
Jools at the back with Chas holding her tightly by the
hand, so she couldn't get closer to take a proper look.
Then they buried Baby Sam by the roadside under a
little stand of trees. No marker, just a sprinkling of
flowers. Ever afterwards, when they passed the spot,
fresh flowers were put there.

They walked in silence till they reached the park
gate. There Meg turned to her and said hesitantly,

'Jools, if you really don't know anything about this Nick Fleming, I'm not sure you ought to go on seeing him.'

'Just in case he turns out to be the smiler with the knife, you mean?'

'No! Nothing like that. It's just . . .'

'Thanks for the advice, Meg. Bye.'

Meg and Nick: as different as day and night. If Meg was going to make her choose between them, then, sorry, Meg! No contest. I'm a night person, too – always have been. We're two of a kind, Nick Fleming and me. We're both night people, living on the edge. Nick Fleming, conjuring pictures out of the empty air! He'd almost had her believing that stuff about vampires – lost, lonely creatures, condemned to wander the earth for all eternity – right down to the way he'd looked at her as he sucked the blood from her finger! Just how a vampire ought to look . . .

She watched Megan until she turned the corner, then let herself into number thirty-four.

There was a buzz of voices from the kitchen, which stopped abruptly as she opened the door. Chas and the Prof were sitting either side of the table.

Chas leapt up. 'Where the hell have you been?'

'School,' said Jools.

'School finished hours ago.'

'I've been with Megan.'

'Didn't it occur to you that I might be worried?'

'No. Why should you be? You know I can look after myself.'

'That's probably what she thought.'

'Who?'

'The girl who was murdered.'

'Her? She looked about as streetwise as Winnie the Pooh – judging from the picture in the paper,' she added quickly.

Chas took a deep breath. 'In future you'll come straight home, or else let me know where you're going to be – and who with.'

Jools looked at him in amazement. 'Since when did you decide to start playing the heavy father?'

'Since you started acting like a thoughtless teenager,' snapped Chas.

'And what's his part in all this?' inquired Jools, indicating the Professor. 'My stepmother? It's him, isn't it? What's he been telling you? That a vampire killed that girl? Don't worry, Chas, I'm protected. By this.' She dangled the little crucifix on its chain in front of him. 'Isn't that right, Professor?'

The Professor stared back at her, unblinking behind his glasses, as if observing a different species.

'That's enough, Jools,' Chas snapped.

The look on his face caught her off-guard. He looked worn out. As calmly as she could, she said, 'There's no need to yell at me. If you're really that worried, we don't have to stay here. We could just pack our bags and go.'

But Chas sank down again into his chair. 'I'm tired, Jools. Leave me alone. We'll talk about it in the morning.'

'Any time,' said Jools, moving to the door. 'Oh, and by the way, you two bozos both stink of garlic!'

It wasn't until she got up to her room that she realised how hungry she was. She couldn't go back downstairs now, not after an exit like that. 'You've been a naughty girl, Jools,' she told herself ruefully, 'so now you'll have to go to bed without any supper.' How very Victorian!

She heard the front door slam as the Professor set off on his nightly wanderings. Soon afterwards came the sound of the clarinet, soft notes creeping up the stairs – 'Solitariness' – but somehow they lost heart before they reached halfway, coiled back on themselves and curled round Chas as he played, shutting her out.

She didn't notice when the music stopped, only the sound of footsteps, stepping briskly and lightly up the stairs, all the way to the top. Not bad for a man who still smoked roll-ups. She'd tried to get him to stop, but that made him cough. You can't play clarinet and cough at the same time. In the end the music always won.

He knocked at the door.

Jools grunted something, which might have been 'Come in.'

In he came. 'I'm sorry,' he said. No fuss, no frills, just 'sorry', leaving her with nothing to say but, 'That's OK. I'm sorry too.'

He sat down on the bed beside her. 'Sorry if I smell of garlic.'

'You don't. Well, perhaps just a bit, sometimes. I lied.'

'Jools, this is stupid. Me sitting downstairs in the warm and you up here in this freezing ivory tower.'

'I like my ivory tower.'

He looked around. 'You've done a good job on it.'

'This is the first time you've seen it, I suppose.'

'Oh! You think the bed makes itself every day? Thanks very much!'

'You haven't tidied up.'

'Forgive me, milady! Did you expect me to? I was afraid I might get my ears bitten off if I so much as moved a pencil, so I've been dusting round things.'

Jools picked up a book at random. It left a neat, book-shaped line of dust behind, like the ghost of a book. 'So you have.' She chuckled.

'*And* I've been going round on my hands and knees with a dustpan and brush, because there's nowhere to plug in the Hoover.' He switched to falsetto, the nagging housewife: 'I've been working my fingers to the bone for you! I've got housemaid's knee and window-cleaner's elbow and bedmaker's back, but do I complain? You bet I do!'

'Shut up, Chas.' She grinned, hugging him.

'Seriously, though,' he said, 'if you're planning to roost up here all winter, I ought to see if I can get a power point put in so you can have an electric fire.'

'We could get an oil stove.'

'Hm. No ventilation. No way out, apart from the door. I don't like that idea. I'll ask Josie if she knows someone.'

'Watch out for Josie. She fancies you.'

'Don't they all?' he remarked placidly. 'Trouble is, every time I go round there, she insists on feeding me. I'm getting a paunch,' he said fretfully, staring down at his stomach.

Jools patted it. 'I think it's sweet. What are you going to call it?'

'Any ideas?'

'Josie, of course, if it's a girl. After all, she is responsible.'

'And if it's a boy?'

'Nick's a nice name. Nicholas.' She said it without thinking.

For a moment the conversation sort of died.

'Everything all right at school?' asked Chas, attempting to restart it.

'Fine.'

'Making friends?'

'A few.'

'Boyfriends?'

'Boys and girls,' she said carefully.

'No one special?'

She shook her head. 'Afraid you might have competition?'

'It's just that Brenda said she saw you with someone.'

'Joseph, I expect.'

'No. This guy was white.'

'You've been talking to Brenda about me?'

'Brenda told Albie and Albie thought it might be someone he knew, and he just happened to mention it to Josie, who—'

'Chinese whispers,' Jools interrupted him. 'It probably *was* Joseph.'

'You could be right.'

Jools swiftly changed the subject. 'Josie's got a great voice.'

'The human voice,' he said softly. 'There's no instrument to match it. I always was a sucker for female singers.'

'Like my mum?'

'Your mum.' He paused. 'Yes. Her voice was a million miles away from Josie's. So soft and warm when she sang, like someone pouring honey on your skin and then licking it off. It still makes my toes curl up, remembering. You know you asked me the other night if you were like her. I was trying to think. You don't look like her. But sometimes, the way you turn your head . . . Or when I'm playing and I catch sight of you in the half-light, listening . . . It could be her.'

Jools broke the silence that followed. 'I don't know how to ask you this, Chas, but I've got to know: she really is dead, isn't she? She didn't just walk out?'

'Oh, yes,' he said quietly. 'She is definitely dead. I had to identify the body.'

She put her arms round him and hugged him tight. 'I'm sorry.'

He said, 'It just felt as if she'd walked out on us. Both of us.'

'You and me.'

'That's right.' He got up. 'Come down when you're ready. I'll put the kettle on. Get you something to eat.'

That evening she worked downstairs at the kitchen table. Chas didn't go out. He sat quietly, letting her study in peace, with the newspaper folded so he could do the crossword. But although he stared at it for over an hour, there were still no more than half a dozen clues filled in, the ones he'd done in the first five minutes.

Jools wasn't concentrating either; she was just running her eyes down each page, mechanically turning one over from time to time . . .

When Mum died, it seemed as if she'd walked out on both of us. That's what he'd said. He didn't mean us. He seemed to be talking about someone else altogether. Some other man? How old was Nick Fleming? Nineteen? Older than she was, anyway. Right! Say there was this other man before Chas came along and Mum had his baby, only Chas didn't know . . .

And then, when I was born, the other man came back. And she couldn't handle it. And then . . . And then . . .

Chas was looking at her, expecting an answer to some question he'd just asked.

'Sorry?' she said.

'I said, if you really want to, we'll go. Move on.'

Jools shook her head. 'I want to stay. Really I do.'

CHAPTER SIX

In the park not a leaf had been left unturned. Every litter bin had been emptied and its contents carted off to be sifted for clues. For the old wino, it was as if his home had been wrecked by vandals. He gathered up his bits and pieces and crept down into Rats' Alley to sleep. And never woke again.

There was just a small paragraph about it on an inside page of the local paper. No foul play suspected. A small death, quite overshadowed by the headlines screaming from the front page: *Second Victim Found*.

The body was discovered lying by the railway line, her head punctually severed by the 5.38 down-train from Paddington. She'd been dead for several hours by then, of multiple knife wounds.

She hadn't been as pretty as the last one, to judge from the photo cut from someone's New Year party snap: pudgy white face in the flashbulb's light; lank hair, a cigarette in one hand and a drink in the other. A girl from the wrong side of the tracks. A single mother who'd left her kids home alone while she worked the night shift at the factory.

'It's almost like they're saying she deserved it,' said Joseph bitterly, as he walked across the park with Jools after school that day.

'No one deserves to die like that,' said Jools.

'The kids were OK. She'd put 'em to bed. That job doesn't pay enough to fork out for a baby-sitter.'

'She told them to bang on the wall if they needed help, right? That's what Chas used to do.'

'Bang on the wall! I s'pose. You'd hear them, any-way, three flats away if they so much as coughed.'

There seemed to be fewer people in the park than usual. Hardly any women on their own. A feeling in the air that bad luck goes in threes. Who'd be next? Please, don't let it be me!

A child's red-and-yellow ball rolled onto the path ahead of them and Jools heard the mother cry out in alarm as the kid broke away from her and came toddling after it. Joseph, hands in his pockets, took a run at the ball, dribbled it, turned, nudged it a few times from one foot to the other, then kicked it back to land at the feet of its awestruck owner.

'She only did it for the kids,' he said, falling into step again beside Jools. 'So they'd have something for Christmas. Last year she borrowed a couple of hundred quid. She was still paying it back, because of the interest. Now they've got nothing, not even their mum.'

They were at the far side of the park now, turning into Park Road.

'Are you coming in?' asked Jools.

Joseph shook his head. 'I gotta get home.'

She frowned. 'Have you been looking after me?'

'I like walking across the park,' he said. 'No problem.'

'Cheers, then.'

'See you.' He turned and walked away. After a few steps he began dribbling an imaginary football.

There were no lights on in number thirty-four that Jools could see, except in the basement kitchen.

Silently she stepped off the path and took a good look through the window to make sure the Prof wasn't there again. Chas was on his own.

For a while she watched him as he set two places at the table, checked the oven, filled the water jug and put out two glasses, giving a final polish to each before he set them down, one, two, so housewifely! His lips were pursed, but there was no sound of whistling: inside his head he could hear the clarinet and every now and then he tried out a bit of the fingering. Beautiful hands, he had. No matter what work he did – gardening, labouring – he'd always looked after his hands. Strange how she'd never noticed before that his hair was going grey, the lines on his face. Strange to think of Chas growing old. Chas was like a rock, unchanging, since the beginning of time – her time. Impossible to imagine that one day he'd die.

You're getting morbid, Jools, she told herself severely. Must be these murders. What do they tell you? Anyone can die, any time. You don't have to be old. So live each moment as it comes.

She walked into the kitchen with a smile on her

face, went straight over to Chas and gave him a hug and a kiss.

'Hey! What's this in aid of?' he exclaimed. 'Is it Christmas already?'

'I love you,' said Jools. 'You're the only dad I've got. And the only mother too. We were just talking about those poor little kids who've got no one now.'

'Love you too, Jools. More than anyone.'

He smelled of soap and cheap tobacco and – 'Mmm! You've been gardening. I can smell it in your hair. And something else, too. Cassoulet for dinner.'

'You can smell that from the oven.'

'Maybe,' said Jools, sniffing again. 'But there's a hint of something extra – like the sweat of your brow labouring over a hot stove. There's an idea for a new line in aftershave! Find out what a girl's favourite food is, then spray on the smell of it cooking! You'd be irresistible!'

'There's just one flaw in that idea,' said Chas, turning to lift the casserole out of the oven. 'Most girls are on a diet these days and trying to avoid the foods they like most.'

'More fools they! Anyway,' she said, as she piled

food onto her plate, 'ask Josie what she thinks you had for dinner. Bet she gets it right.'

'Actually,' he said, 'I was thinking of giving her a buzz. Tell the lads I can't make it tonight.'

'Whatever for?'

'I don't know. The Prof says—'

'Oh, the Prof!'

'I just get a bad feeling sometimes about leaving you on your own so much.'

'I'm OK. The band need you. No one's going to get in here without me opening the door. I'll be all right. Just go.'

By the time they'd finished eating, she'd persuaded him. He left her with a final warning about not opening the door to anyone.

'Like who, for instance?'

He gave her an apologetic look and went.

Jools spread out her books on the table, but she couldn't settle. The trouble with working downstairs in the warm was that there was bound to be some book upstairs in her room that she needed. Off she went in search of it, without quite knowing which one she wanted.

With her pencil held between her teeth, she leafed through the books on her shelves, one after the other, until she was close enough to the window to see down into the street below.

There stood Nick Fleming, waiting patiently under the streetlamp for her to notice him. Romeo and Juliet. She could see his lips moving, as she recalled the lines:

But soft! what light through yonder window breaks?
It is the east and Juliet is the sun.

He nodded towards the door and she ran down the stairs to open it, just a crack, peering round. 'Chas told me not to open the door to anyone,' she said.

'You could let me in through the window, I suppose. There's no one else at home?'

'No one.' She opened the door wide. 'You'd better come in, if you're coming.'

'How could I resist such a charming invitation?' He walked straight past her and flung open first the door on the left – 'Hm! Fifties nostalgia,' he remarked, 'not my favourite period' – then the door of the study,

'Woh! This is unreal!' Not that there was much to see, until she switched on the light, but Nick was already entranced by the stuffed animals and birds, moving swiftly from one to another, bending down to address a fox, stretching his arms as he rose up towards the owl, mimicking its wings spread wide. Wherever he moved, the effect was magical, animals no longer standing alone but shifting into groups or pairs, heads turned, ears cocked, a paw or a wing lifted to emphasize a point. He hardly seemed to touch them: it was as if he'd simply breathed new life into them and they'd decided to throw a party to celebrate.

Satisfied with the effect he had created, he turned his attention to the shelves of dusty books. 'What have we got here? The old boy's life work?' His fingers danced over the spines until one or another caught his fancy and he'd pull it out, blow off the dust and riffle through the pages before dismissing it – 'Madame Blavatsky! Dear old fraud!' He tossed the book aside. Jools fielded it and tucked it back on the shelf. 'What else have we got? *Varney the Vampire, or the Feast of Blood.* Such rubbish! *Malleus Maleficarum* – he certainly has covered the field. Here's Montague Summers.' He opened the book, apparently at random, and began to declaim: '"In all the darkest pages of the malign supernatural there is no more horrible tradition than that of the vampire, a pariah even among demons."' He laughed. 'How many demons did he canvass for their opinion, I wonder?'

'Nick! I think you ought to stop.'

'And these pictures! Look! If vampires looked like this, they'd never pass muster in polite society.'

'Please, Nick!' She rescued another couple of books from the floor, but it was getting impossible to keep up with his progress, or to put them back in their proper places.

'The point about vampires, sweet Juliette, is that they look exactly like you and me.'

'If they set about wrecking people's houses the moment they're inside, they still won't get invited in.'

'You're right, of course,' he agreed cheerfully. 'Never mind. We'll clear up later.'

'What if the Prof comes back now?'

'He won't. He's busy on the other side of town.'

'How do you know?'

'I just know. I wonder where he keeps his diary?' He began searching through the drawers of the desk, expertly, starting at the bottom, leaving them open.

'Nick! You can't read someone's private diary.'

'I mean the record of his researches. Aren't you curious about what he gets up to during all his nightly ramblings?'

'No! Now help me put this lot back before I throw you out.'

'OK. There's nothing interesting here anyway.' Together they scooped up the last of the books, bundled them back on the shelves, and tidied the drawers into some sort of order. The animals they left as they were. They looked good. Besides, Jools hadn't the faintest idea how they'd been arranged to start with. She dragged Nick out of the room and closed the door behind them.

'I'll just take a quick look upstairs while I'm here,' he said. And he was off again, taking the stairs two at a time, peering into the Professor's bedroom, opening the wardrobe, poking his head round the door of the little bathroom, pausing briefly to sniff the air.

Then he was trying the door on the other side of the landing. 'What's in here?'

'Nothing,' said Jools. 'It's always locked.'

'I daresay the key's not far away.' He looked around, keen eyes searching for possible hiding places.

'He keeps it in his pocket.'

'Hm.' He crossed to the bedroom door and took out the key. 'In these old houses,' he explained, 'quite often all the locks are the same. Let's see.' He fitted the key into the lock. It turned.

'Please, Nick! I don't think we should.'

'Don't you want to know what's inside?'

'I'm not sure I do.' What was she expecting to find? Bluebeard's Castle? Corpses of all his past wives hanging on hooks on the wall? Certainly not what she did see, when he beckoned her to look.

A bedroom. The prettiest room in the whole house, with pink flowered wall paper, pink coverlet and curtains. Pictures of fluffy animals and china ornaments, souvenirs of seaside towns. The wardrobe, when he opened it, was chock-full of women's clothes and hats and shoes, in the styles of forty or more years ago. On the dressing-table

Jools found a wedding photograph, the bridegroom, in British Army uniform, clearly recognisable as the Professor, with his old-young face.

'Taken in Vienna, I'd say,' said Nick, when she showed it to him. 'Just after the war.'

'So that's his wife,' murmured Jools.

'Liesl,' he said softly, still staring at the photograph.

'How did you know her name?'

'It's written on the back here.' He turned it over to show her. 'Armin. Liesl. April 1946.'

Jools moved to the open window, breathing in the night air. She said, 'I've heard him so many times, standing at this window, saying her name over and over again, as if he can't believe she's dead. As if one evening he'll turn round and find her standing there. He's kept her room as a sort of shrine all this time.'

'The way I heard it,' Nick said, with a chuckle, 'she ran off with an insurance salesman to live in Clacton-on-Sea. Perhaps he prefers to think of her as dead.'

'Can we go down now, please?'

As they came out of the room, he nodded towards the attic stairs. 'What's up there?'

'Just the attics. A junk room and my bedroom. And I'm not inviting you up there. Certainly not, in this mood.'

'OK.' He locked the door behind them and put the key back where it belonged.

He let her take him by the hand and lead him downstairs to the kitchen. 'Your hands are freezing,' she said.

'Are they? I don't feel the cold.'

She opened the door of the stove to let out more heat. 'Coffee?'

'No, thanks. You go ahead.'

Nick settled himself in Chas's chair, suddenly lethargic, staring into the fire.

Jools sat on the stool at his feet. 'You never finished your story,' she said.

'My story?' He seemed almost to have forgotten she was there.

'The three vampires – though they're down to two now. The young one went mad, you said, killing without mercy, indiscriminately. Those two poor girls!' she added, suddenly reminded.

He shook his head seriously. 'No vampire did that.'

'Of course, you're the expert on vampires.'

'It was too messy! A knife, stabbing over and over again, finding the heart almost by chance! A vampire needs no weapons but his hands and teeth. These women fought for their lives. A vampire would have given them no time: if he has a mind to kill, a vampire can strike faster than the eye can see. A vampire is strong. Look at me, Juliette! If I were a vampire and I put my hands either side of your head – like this – with one quick jerk it would be all over. But dead blood is useless to a vampire. To drink from the living, the best way is first to hypnotise his prey. Look at me,' his voice became softer, gentler. 'They feel no fear, Juliette. No pain. The blood tastes better that way and he can take his time . . . All he wants is the chance to share a human life, just for a little while . . . The thoughts and memories . . . the hopes and fears . . . Where's the harm in that? Wake up now!' He snapped his fingers.

'I wasn't asleep,' said Jools.

'No?'

'I just felt a bit giddy for a moment.'

'What was the last thing you remember me saying?'

He was laughing at her, teasing her — but, oh! those sea-green eyes! Eyes that could change in a moment from sparkling mischief to a sadness fathoms deep. What was the last thing he'd said?

'I refuse to answer that. Whatever I say, you can always claim to have said something else. Why don't you get on with the story?'

'But this is all part of the story. I am explaining to you that the trail of a vampire is hard to follow. His victims have no memory of what has happened, except a slight weakness, which soon passes. He kills only when he is threatened. But our young vampire was out of control, draining the life from each one, killing all those who stood in his way. So Flamel tracked his son from town to town by the number of sudden unexplained deaths among the young and fit. The vicious murders of those who tried to protect them. But already the trail was growing fainter. Our vampire was losing his taste for death because, in the end, all deaths are the same. There is always that final moment of perfect peace, like a tiny taste of heaven . . .' With a wry smile he said, 'He'd got around to reading the small print, as you put it. You said there had to be a catch? It was so simple. No soul means no death, so no reckoning to be made, ever, no heaven or hell – or so you'd think. But with every death came this small, indescribably sweet taste of heaven, and he realised—' He took a deep breath and, staring into the red glow of the fire, slowly recited:

> *'Why, this is Hell, nor am I out of it.*
> *Think you that I, that saw the face of God*
> *And tasted the eternal joys of Heaven,*
> *Am not tormented with ten thousand hells*
> *In being deprived of everlasting bliss?'*

'You understand?' he asked softly. 'To have tasted heaven and know you're for ever shut out – that's hell. He was already in hell. For ever. It was hell or nothing. Pernelle, in the end, chose to be nothing.'

There was a long silence.

'Why didn't he do the same?' Jools asked at last.

'Finish it? Like Pernelle?' He paused for thought, then answered quietly and simply, 'He was afraid.' Suddenly he tensed, listening. 'There's someone outside the window. Go and look.'

Obediently Jools got up and went to the window, but even with her nose pressed up against the glass there was little to see, without turning off the light.

'Too late,' said Nick. 'He's moving round the side of the house now.'

'I can't hear anything.'

'Sh! It's the Professor.'

'But you said—'

'Perhaps I was wrong about him.'

Then she heard the key in the lock. There was a faint stirring of the air inside the house as the front door opened and closed again. The Professor's shuffling footsteps moved towards the stairs: up or down?

'Will he come down here?' whispered Nick.

Jools shook her head. 'Chas always leaves him something to eat in the dining-room.'

She recognised the creak of the bedroom stairs, slightly muffled by carpet. Strange how she'd never noticed before how different they sounded from the bare boards of the stairs coming down to the basement. Above them, a door opened and closed.

'Time to go, I think,' said Nick.

Jools said, 'I'll come up and close the front door after

you. With luck he won't hear.' What did it matter if he did? She could have friends in if she wanted, couldn't she? But Nick's tension was catching.

Hand in hand they crept up the stairs. As they reached the top, a door opened again and Nick shrank back into the shadows as light spilled down the stairwell.

The Professor's voice called, 'Chas! Is that you?'

'It's me,' Jools answered, trying to keep her voice level.

'Ah! Miss Julie. Is Chas with you?'

'No.'

'Strange. I thought I saw him with you in the kitchen.'

(Nosy old spook!) 'Chas is out. Is there anything you want? I can get it for you.'

Out of the corner of her eye, she saw Nick shaking his head.

From above, the voice came again, 'No, thank you. There is nothing you can get for me. Goodnight.'

'Night!'

As soon as the door closed and the light was gone,

Nick moved out of the shadows and caught hold of her arm. 'Let's both go out!'

'Go where?'

'Anywhere!'

'Let me get my coat, then.'

Swiftly she clattered back down the stairs, checked the fire, snatched up her coat and, with one half-regretful look at her homework (but it didn't have to be in till Monday), turned out the light.

It was good to be out in the street, breathing fresh air. Sitting alone in the house wasn't so bad, but having the Professor shuffling about gave her the creeps.

CHAPTER SEVEN

They made their way along rain-wet streets, past tiny Victorian terraces, two-up, two-down, and shops to scale. Not chainstores like those on the smart side of town, but proper shops, a second-hand-book shop and an ironmonger's, a watch-repairer's and a corner shop, still open, though it must be nine o'clock. There were even a few market stalls, selling flowers and fruit and spices, brassware and Indian jewellery. Enticing smells floated out of restaurant doorways, Indian, Turkish, Thai, Vietnamese, Caribbean. Voices in half a dozen different languages. This is where we should have lived, thought Jools. This is where we belong.

Outside an antique shop, one of those few where among the clutter you might just stumble across a real bargain, Nick suddenly stopped. 'Isn't he beautiful?' he breathed.

His gaze was fixed on a rocking-horse that took up most of the window. It was delicately painted a dapple-grey, the saddle and harness lovingly restored, the mane and tail made of real horsehair. With his forehead pressed up against the window-pane, he whispered so softly that his breath didn't so much as mist up the glass,

'*I had a little pony. His name was Dapple Grey. I lent him to a lady*—'

'Nick?' She tugged at his arm. 'What is it?'

'Nothing. A memory I used to have a pony. Long ago. When I was little. I called him Dapple Grey – like in the nursery rhyme. Do you know, I still miss him? Every child should have a pet. Something to love. Some creature that loves him, quite unconditionally. Even if, to a stranger's eyes, it's just a lump of wood. Come on!' He was suddenly striding away again, down dark streets and narrow passageways, then across the main road at the traffic-lights and she realised where they were heading. The Spotted Cow, of course, but approaching from the back way, through the carpark, past the lighted window of the kitchen.

For the second time that evening Jools stopped to watch Chas without him knowing she was there. He was standing by the door, chatting to Josie, who was at the table, buttering home-baked rolls. No ready-sliced bread for Josie's customers, or frozen veg. Her home-made soup was a meal in itself for a starving man.

It was like watching a play with the sound turned down.

Chas moved in closer, said something else and Josie smiled and bent to fetch a tray of sausages out of the oven. As she began transferring them to a plate, Chas reached out to take one and she slapped his wrist. But while she was hanging up her apron, he snatched up a sausage and bit into it before she could tell him to put it back. Too late he discovered it was still piping hot and rushed to the sink for a glass of water.

Josie, laughing, was all motherly concern, getting him to put out his tongue: *Let me see. Hm. You'll live. Teach you to be greedy.*

A brief kiss, as if they were too used to kissing to

make a big thing of it, then they took the plates of food and went out together.

Jools felt Nick's arms around her, his hair brushing her cheek. 'A pretty scene,' he whispered. 'So homely.'

Chas and Josie. Why should she care about Chas and Josie? She'd long ago lost count of Chas's girlfriends, over the years . . .

Nick went on, 'You've never cared before because he always leaves them, doesn't he? Before he gets too involved. But you're afraid that this time it might be different.'

'He talked about me – maybe – going to university.' She remembered what she'd said then: 'Are you trying to get rid of me?' Only joking.

'Sooner or later,' Nick said, 'one of you is going to have to make the break. Why should you hang around waiting for him to do it?'

She noticed again the odd fact that he didn't smell of anything at all. His body, close against her, was neither warmer nor colder than her own. It was like having another, stronger self, wrapped round her, keeping her safe.

Jools stood lost in thought. She didn't notice him slip away, leaving her alone in the darkness, with no choice but to go inside.

The band was running through a final number before breaking for beer and sausages. 'I can't give you anything but love, baby'. Josie was belting out the words, with plenty of meaningful looks at Chas, but Chas's playing was all over the place. He managed to busk it until they came to his solo. There he played a few bars, lost the thread, tried again, then, with an apologetic shrug, nodded to Ninja to take over, who wasn't ready . . . Seeing Jools come in gave them all a good excuse to stop.

'I finished what had to be done tonight,' she told Chas. 'Then I felt lonely.' She'd missed out a whole chunk of what had happened in between, but lonely was how she felt now. And Chas, instead of bawling her out for walking through the dark streets alone, looked at her hard and said, 'You look a bit pale. Is everything OK?'

'I'm fine.' He gave her a quick kiss on the forehead and led her over to join the others.

'Kids, eh!' remarked Ninja with a grin. 'Anywhere there's food!'

Jools glared at him and went to sit by Joseph.

'What's up with Chas?' Joseph asked her.

'He burned his mouth,' Jools said sourly. 'Serve him right.'

'That's two of us having a bad evening.' He heaved a sigh. 'I was having a go on the piano before you came in. It's not going to work.'

Jools said, 'Why not? The three of you – you, Chas and Albie – sounded pretty good to me that first afternoon in the bar.'

'Bum notes and all?'

She nodded. 'Bum notes and all. Why don't you three play a short set – towards the end of the first half, say? Give Dave and Ninja a bit of extra drinking time and they won't complain.'

'Bit different from the rest of what we're doing.'

'So spread your wings a little. Find your own style. Chas'll back you up. Want me to have a word with him?'

He smiled. 'Thanks, Jools.'

'Maybe not tonight, though. Give his tongue a chance to heal.'

As she and Chas were walking home, they saw the police cars down the side-street and the tapes stretched across the pavement, preventing the small knot of people that had gathered from getting any closer to the corner shop. It would have been against human nature to walk past and ignore it. You had to find out if what you already half knew was true . . .

Another girl murdered! An Indian girl, left in charge of her father's shop as she was every evening. She should have been safe enough, with the rest of the family just upstairs and the lights full on – anyone might have come in!

Several people had, while she lay there, hidden behind the stacks of shelves. Most had lingered for a while, wondering why there was no one to serve them, and gone away empty-handed. Some – at least three – had taken what they needed and left the money in a neat pile on the counter. The ones who would be hardest to track down were those who hadn't bothered to pay. At last, one old lady, more persistent than the rest, had gone searching for some assistance and stepped in something sticky. She said she thought at first that someone had dropped a jar of jam.

Why hadn't the girl cried out for help? The police pathologist pursed his lips: some kind of ligature about the windpipe? Her own scarf, possibly (a long, silky thing). She'd been so badly hacked about, it was impossible to say without a proper post-mortem.

All this the eager onlookers pieced together from phrases overheard, fleshed out with bits of information passed on by the young constable stationed by the tape, who would have known better if he hadn't been a bit over-excited, this being his first murder. The old lady who'd found the body was mainly concerned about whether she'd left the kettle on when she slipped out for a pint of milk: could Vera go and check? Came out in her slippers, she did, and look at them now – ruined! The blood on the fluffy trimming provided quite a talking point before the police carried them away in a plastic bag for forensic examination, leaving her in a pair of borrowed wellingtons.

Perhaps the girl knew her attacker. That's why she

hadn't cried out. Took him round the corner by the biscuits for a quick kiss and a cuddle. And then—

This her father vigorously denied. 'My daughter was a good girl. No menfriends. She worked. She studied. She helped her mother. She served in the shop. Too busy she was to have boyfriends. She was not one of these girls who are always out to parties, taking drugs, wandering the streets alone without telling us where she is going.'

Jools felt Chas's arm tighten round her when he said that. She couldn't repress a shudder, for a different reason. She'd been in no danger: she'd been with Nick when she'd passed the shop. Had the girl been alive then? She cast her mind back, trying to remember if she'd seen anyone inside. There could have been a dozen people hidden by the shelves – or else just one, the murderer.

Inevitably the phrase was bandied about: serial killer. The young constable was quick to quash that idea. They weren't looking for a serial killer yet, he said knowledgeably: to qualify as a serial killer, you have to kill at least four people – preferably five. Which wasn't much comfort to anyone, really.

*   *   *

"'Talk you of killing? Then heaven have mercy on me!'" warbled Tanith aka Desdemona, twitching suggestively at the long chiffon scarf she'd taken to wearing recently – a bit tasteless, in view of what had happened to the girl in the Indian corner shop, but taste, rather than fashion, had never been Tanith's strong point.

"'Think on thy sins!'" boomed Ms Eng. Lit., who'd decided she was the only person to read Othello, after trying out all three boys in the class and finding them a bit low on passion.

Tanith was playing Desdemona for the third lesson running. While the two of them gave it the full monty, boredom settled over the rest of the class like a great black carrion bird.

"'Kill me tomorrow!'" pleaded Tanith. "'Let me live tonight!'"

"'Nay, an you strive . . .'" chimed in Ms Eng. Lit. (who probably didn't know what she meant either).

"'But half an hour, while I say one prayer!'"

But would you give your soul? mused Jools. I don't think so! And what about Iago? Why did he do it? Destroy four innocent people – or was it five? They'd had a long discussion about that, a few lessons back. Jealousy? someone had suggested. Frustrated ambition? Because Cassio got promoted over him (and Cassio was, quite frankly, an upper-class twit, as well as an alkie). Four people dead because he missed his promotion? Wasn't that a bit OTT? Racial prejudice, then? Boredom? someone yawned.

Jools said, out of the blue, 'He did it because he could, right? He didn't have to have a reason.'

Ms Eng. Lit. answered, 'I think that's a rather *modern* way of thinking, don't you, Jools? For Shakespeare. A bit existentialist.'

After that Jools shut up, let them get on with it.

Iago, the man without a soul. No sense of right or wrong, good or bad. A kind of vampire, draining the energy from the people around him. Othello's supposed to be the hero, but Iago's the one in control. He's the one you watch. Iago is sexy.

'You hear about Mo's kids?' Joseph asked Jools as he walked her home across the park that evening.

'Who's Mo?'

'The girl who was killed.'

'Oh. The second girl? What happened to them?'

'Nothing bad. Pretty good, actually. A van came round with a load of toys. I told you she was only working so she could get them something for Christmas. I tell you, it was like Mo's dream-list. Man United strip and new boots – designer trainers – CD player! Must have been a thousand quid's worth, even without the rocking-horse.'

'The what?'

'I'm telling you no lie, man. A rocking-horse, real antique! Must be some rich old guy who felt sorry for them . . .'

'Why old?'

'Only an old guy would think of buying them a rocking-horse.' He laughed. 'They have to climb over it to get into bed.'

'But do they like it?'

'Can't get the little 'un off it till he's asleep.'

Jools smiled to herself, remembering Nick's face, pressed up against the shop window. 'What colour is it?'

'Sort of spotted, their nan said. Grey and white.'

'Dapple-grey,' said Jools. 'I don't think I'll go home yet. There's something I want to check.'

'Want me to come with you?'

'If you like.'

In the fading daylight the Victorian terraced houses looked mean and squat, the shops dusty and crammed with stuff that no one wanted to buy. The blinds were down at the Indian corner shop. Three or four cheap bunches of flowers lay awkwardly on the step, as if they weren't sure whether they ought to have come.

Jools walked on till she reached the antique shop. Two ugly dining chairs now filled the window. She pushed open the door and went inside. Joseph teetered on the step for a moment, then dived in after her.

'What happened to the rocking-horse?' she asked the man behind the counter.

'Sold it, love. Sorry.'

'That's all right. I think it might be a friend of mine who bought it. An old man.'

He shook his head. 'No, a youngster.'

'Did he give you his name? An address?'

'Paid cash. Had it collected. Who's asking?'

Jools wished she was old enough or smart enough to pretend she was some kind of a detective. She shrugged. 'I just thought if he was planning to sell it on, my friend might make him an offer. Never mind. Come on, Joseph.'

'What was all that about?' asked Joseph as soon as they were outside.

'Just an idea.'

'Same one the Old Bill had. Just to save you going to the sports shop and the toyshop and the firm he got to deliver, it was a young guy, long hair tied back in a ponytail. That's about all anyone remembers. Always paid cash. They went back and asked the old lady if it sounded like anyone she knew. A young guy with a thousand quid to spend on someone else's kids? Oh, yes, she said, this estate's full of them. Said it was the first laugh she'd had since Mo died.'

'Probably just fronting for your rich old eccentric,' said Jools.

There was no doubt in her mind that the young man was Nick. The hungry look on his face as he'd stared at the rocking-horse in the antique shop window! Longing to buy it, make some kid happy – even a stranger's kids. A thousand quid's worth, though. Mo's dream-list. How could he have known about that, unless . . .?

She wasn't a stranger.

Nor was the first girl.

What about the Indian girl from the corner shop? No boyfriends, her father had said, but you could tell by the way the neighbours looked at one another when he said that that they knew better. Not a going-out-to-discos boyfriend, maybe, but just a customer, who came into the shop more often than he needed to, whenever she happened to be there. Someone who brought a smile to her face and made her heart beat faster.

Three out of three still wouldn't mean he'd killed them. What was it he'd said, when they'd talked about the murders? Too messy. If Nick was going to kill someone, he'd do it with style. What was she thinking? Of course he hadn't killed them. That was just the way it looked to her because she could see a connection no one else could. Let's keep it that way.

'You OK?' asked Joseph.

'I'm fine,' she said.

CHAPTER EIGHT

There was some talk of cancelling the school Hallowe'en dance, until it was discovered that the young sociology teacher, who'd been lumbered with the job of organising it, had let his enthusiasm carry him away into paying for the disco in full in advance.

The Head made the best of a bad job by calling the sixth form into the hall and treating them like adults. Said she was sure they were all quite aware of the dangers of letting any of the girls walk to or from the dance on their own. She trusted them to make sure no one was put in that situation. If anyone had a problem, members of staff would be there on the night, with their cars, to provide free transport. A few anxious parents still refused to fork out for tickets, but sales weren't much down on previous years.

There was consternation among the acolytes when

Tanith hinted that she might not be coming. Quite apart from the fact that that would leave them in a quandary as to whether they ought to come themselves, they were dying to get a look at Tanith's new boyfriend. She'd dropped all sorts of hints about a flash car and money to burn, but she wouldn't even tell them his name, just twitched at her long scarf suggestively whenever the subject came up. What was she hiding under that scarf? Love-bites, maybe?

Tanith only twitched at the scarf some more, with what she thought of as an enigmatic smile. Jools thought she looked more like a constipated hen, but that was just her opinion.

'Pumpkin heads and trick-or-treat, that's kids' stuff,' scoffed Tanith. 'And dressing up as ghosts and witches – bor-ing!'

'I agree with Tanith,' the sociology teacher said, much to everyone's surprise. 'Witches, whatever, are a bit old hat. That's not what it's supposed to be about at all. Hallowe'en is All Saints' Eve, the old pagan feast of Samhain, when the souls of the dead return to walk among the living – so lay an extra place at

121

the table, Mother, just in case! Sit by the churchyard gate at midnight and you may see the souls pass by of all those marked down to die in the coming year – if you dare to take the risk of seeing your own face among them. Take care that young man or woman you meet doesn't turn out to be one of the Fair Folk – never make the mistake of calling them fairies, silly little will-o'-the-wisp creatures. These are the Old Ones, the Lordly Ones, who move among us unseen all the rest of the year. But on Hallowe'en, when the way between their world and ours is open, they can carry you off to the hollow hills from which you'll emerge next day to find that centuries have passed and all those you love are dead and gone.' He got quite lyrical about it. 'Hallowe'en is the night when you can begin to become the person you want to be – the person you already are inside – a pop star, or a scientist, or a nurse . . . even a teacher,' he added, with a wry smile, 'though I wouldn't recommend it. That's what the dressing up is really about. Sort of sympathetic magic. "This is who I am!" Say it loud enough and you can make it happen!'

Tanith thought about it.

'Of course, it takes a bit of courage to take that first step,' he added.

A slow smile spread over Tanith's face. At last she nodded. 'OK,' she said.

Jools had no trouble deciding what she was going as. She was going as herself, in the jacket Lady Rachel had made for her under instructions from Baby Sam.

'That'll make a change,' Chas remarked. She was hardly ever out of that jacket, these days.

'I'm me,' said Jools. 'That's who I want to be. I don't want to change.'

'Fair enough. Most girls enjoy dressing up.'

On the evening of the disco, Chas walked with her across the park to the school. 'Now,' he said, 'have you decided what you're going to do about getting home?'

'Don't worry. I'll make sure I get an escort.'

'Someone you know.'

'Of course.'

'You get any problems, you can ring me at the

pub any time up to eleven-thirty. You've got Josie's number?'

'Trust me, Dad.'

She never called him Dad. He backed off. 'See you later, then.'

Little knots of people stood around outside the gate, chatting, smoking or waiting for friends.

Once inside, she wasn't surprised to see that a certain number had gone for the soft option, borrowing stuff from their friends and relations – nurses, professors, part-time soldiers.

But then there were the others – the gypsies, the folk singers, the big-game hunters: *Look at me! This is who I want to be. This is who I am inside. This is the real me.* Helen of Troy, with her teeth in braces. Two burglars in masks and stripy jerseys, his and hers – no wonder Ms Eng. Lit. despaired of the youth of today. But to redress the balance there were also at least two Mrs Thatcher look-alikes. If you asked any of them outright, they'd shrug it off, play it cool: 'This? It's just something to wear . . .'

Sporting Hero was wearing his rugby kit, so no change there.

If he hadn't been taking the tickets as they came in, Jools never would have recognised the sociology teacher under his clown's make-up. He had on one of those sad-happy faces. She'd never think of him in quite the same way again. Even Ms Eng. Lit. had entered into the spirit of things. She was dressed like a Victorian granny, in black bombazine with a widow's cap, wistfully harking back to an age when life was simpler and young people respected their elders and betters.

A few people either hadn't got the message or else had decided to ignore it and turned up in traditional Hallowe'en gear. It was just possible their secret wish was to be a witch or a vampire. Maybe the girl in skin-tight black with a skeleton painted on it was making a philosophical statement: *This is what we all become, whether we want to or not.* Two sad zombies looked as if they might be having second thoughts: they were stuck in this make-up for the duration and would probably have to spend the evening dancing with each other.

The really canny ones had just slipped on a lab coat over their mufti. Later on, they could slip it off again, meanwhile, they could have it both ways . . .

'Which are you supposed to be, Joseph?' Jools asked him. 'A Hammer-horror mad scientist or a serious Nobel-Prize contender?'

Joseph grinned self-consciously, looking down at his white coat. 'You mean this? My mum's idea. She thinks I should be a doctor.'

'Is that what you want to be?'

'I dunno. A nurse, maybe. Children's nurse. I got enough of them to practise on at home. Come on. Let's dance. What was that step you were doing the other day in the park?'

'That was a slip jig. You can't do that to this.'

'Wanna bet? Four-four time, right?'

Somehow he managed it. He danced it all the way down the hall until he fetched up with a bunch of his mates who were showing off to their girls.

As Jools made to follow him, she caught a glimpse of Nick Fleming, in a plain dark suit and white open-necked shirt. Like her, he'd seen no need for fancy dress. He was who he wanted to be. Then she lost sight of him again. What was he doing here? Someone

126

must have bought him a ticket. She followed the way he seemed to be heading, back to the entrance, past a belly-dancer talking to a guy in a gorilla suit. Strange ambitions some people have.

She was just in time to see Tanith sail in, towing in her wake a guy in a DJ, bow tie and fancy waistcoat, who looked as if he'd rather be anywhere but here as the fan club clustered round.

'Are we very late?' asked Tanith, adding loudly enough for everyone in sight to hear, 'Patrick insisted on taking me for a bite to eat first at the Country Club.'

She'd dyed her hair black for the occasion and painted her face near-white with a scarlet slash of lipstick. As she shrugged off her coat, the fan club gasped in admiration. Even Jools gave a quick intake of breath at the sight of the Princess Caraboo metamorphosed into Morticia Addams, in a low-cut black dress that swept the floor, her scarf a blood-red gash across her throat and trailing down her back. Tanith, the would-be vamp: that figured.

'Come along, Patrick,' she said, taking him firmly by the hand and leading him towards the dancing. As they passed her, Jools heard her add more quietly, 'It's just for half an hour, poppet. Then we'll go on somewhere more interesting.'

At last things were warming up in the hall. The music grew rapidly louder, thumping, rhythmic, repetitive, until it was impossible to talk. Nothing to do but dance. Impossible even to think, except to wonder vaguely why she'd wanted to come. She told herself irritably that the feeling would pass; that she always felt this way around this point in the evening. If she could just get out into the fresh air for a bit and clear her head . . .

But security on the door was tight: no girls were being allowed out on their own, to risk becoming another murder victim. The classrooms were supposed to be off-limits, too, but she set off anyway, through echoing, dusty corridors, in and out of the patches of moonlight shafting through the windows, until the music faded into the distance and there was nothing but an ultrasonic thump-thump-thump, felt rather than heard. Sometimes she caught the sound of voices, briefly – more refugees sheltering from that barrage of sound. Then silence again.

She stood for a while at a window, looking out across the centre courtyard, watching the scene in the hall opposite. Lights flashed red and blue and green. Figures bobbed up and down, like parts of some bizarre machine. It seemed so far away – too far to go back. She was free – free to feel the charge of excitement in the air about her, like the build-up of electricity before a storm, drawing in energy from all around. She could hear the scuffle of feet, all hurrying in the same direction, and a whisper of voices.

Light spilled from the doorway of the art room. A small crowd had gathered inside, clustered round a table in the centre. Jools climbed onto a bench at the back so she could get a better look. Around her, wire armatures hung from the ceiling, half-covered in papier-mâché, like the skeletons of prehistoric birds. African-style masks, made out of seeds and pasta, gazed down from the walls at Nick Fleming, sitting with three girls, as if playing cards. The crowd watched his every move as he shuffled the pack, so casually, his eyes on the girls, smiling faintly, holding their attention. His coat and shirt sleeves were pushed back as far as they would go – *See? Nothing up my sleeves.*

Opposite her, Jools watched Tanith, red lips parted, blood-red fingernails digging into Patrick's arm, as Nick offered the pack of cards to the first girl to cut, then shuffled it again. He repeated this action with the second girl and the third. Then he dealt four hands.

The crowd watched, disbelieving, as the first girl turned up her hand, to show all thirteen hearts, in order, from the ace to the king. He nodded to the second girl, who held all the clubs. The third held diamonds. Nick's own hand? Spades, of course, in order, like the rest.

There was a ripple of applause, which was suddenly cut short as Patrick, like a man with a mission (seek and destroy, at a guess), elbowed his way forward exclaiming harshly, 'So that's how you did it! You jammy little oik!'

'Did what?' Nick asked sociably, gathering up the cards.

'Took more than a grand off me when we were playing the other night!'

'The other night?' Nick frowned. Then he looked up and smiled. 'Oh, it's you, Patrick. I didn't recognise you in the fancy dress. Love the waist-coat!'

'You cheated me!'

'We played cards. You lost. Quite heavily, as I remember.' As Nick was speaking, he idly cut the cards one-handed – once, twice, three, four times – and dealt himself four kings.

'You're a card-sharp!'

'That's a serious accusation where I come from,' Nick said pleasantly.

Patrick stood his ground. 'I want my money back.'

'Sorry. No can do. I spent it. Anyway, I didn't cheat. I didn't need to. You play like a fool, Patrick. I'll play you now, if you like – and beat you. I won't even touch the cards again. Let someone else deal.'

'I'll deal,' said Tanith, pushing one of the girls out of the way so she could take her chair. 'What are you playing?'

Nick passed her the cards, but Patrick, after a pause, shook his head. 'I won't play with you. There's bound to be a catch.'

Nick shrugged, pushed back his chair and stood up.

'OK. If that's how you feel. But just to show there are no hard feelings . . . Fan out the cards,' he told Tanith. Then he nodded to Patrick. 'Pick a card.' He held up his hands. 'See? I haven't touched them.'

The audience stood waiting.

Patrick, reluctantly, took a card.

'And now I turn my back,' said Nick, suiting the action to the words. 'Look at the card, Patrick. Memorise it. Just to be sure, why don't you write your name on it? Lend him a pen, someone. Go on, Patrick. You do know how to write your name? If not, a cross will do. Finished? Now, put the card back in the pack.' He turned again to face them. 'If I can't pick out your card, Patrick, I promise you'll get your money back, every penny. The odds against me are fifty-one to one. That should be good enough even for you. Just to make it a bit more interesting . . .' He snapped his fingers and a knife appeared in his hand, a wicked little stiletto.

Several people stepped back quickly onto the toes of those behind them.

Nick nodded to Tanith, and watched as she spread out the cards on the table. He glanced up at Patrick.

Then the knife flashed through the air and landed, quivering, skewering one card.

'Is that your card?' asked Nick.

Patrick's fingers closed round the handle of the knife and he pulled it free. He picked up the card with his left hand, glanced at it, flung it face up on the table, so that they could all see the signature scrawled across it, then shot a look of fury at Nick and tensed himself, tightening his grip on the knife.

What happened next happened so fast . . . Some people said afterwards they'd seen Nick vault across the table and seize the knife before Patrick had it firmly in his grasp. Though to do that, he would have had to move faster than the eye could see . . . Somehow the knife was in Nick's hand again, the point at Patrick's throat.

'Not fast enough, little man!' hissed Nick. 'You'll have to move quicker than that to take me!'

Then a voice from the door demanded: 'What is going on in here?' It was Ms Eng. Lit., a fury in black bombazine. 'Is either of you young men a pupil at this school? Then I suggest you both leave, or I shall have to call the police.'

'No problem,' said Nick amiably, slipping the knife back in his pocket. 'We were going anyway. Tanith!' He didn't even glance in her direction, simply held out his hand, knowing that she would take it.

'Sorry, Patrick.' She shrugged. 'You've cut your pretty face, too.' With one finger she skimmed off the blood and licked it clean. 'Mm! Dinner was – delicious.'

It was quite an exit the two of them made, Nick pausing to plant a kiss on the lips of Ms Eng. Lit., which left her too dizzy to protest as the rest streamed past her, because where Tanith went, there the fan club followed, together with their boyfriends and assorted hangers-on. Even as she felt herself swept along with the crowd, Jools was thinking: This has to be a set-up! They'd planned it between them, Nick and Tanith. Tanith never had any intention of spending her evening at a boring old school disco, or with that fool Patrick. What next? Where were they all going now? Down the corridor they ran, collecting more followers along with their coats, then on and out of the building.

'Where are you going, Jools?' she heard Joseph cry.

'I don't know!' she called back. 'Somewhere much more fun than here!'

Then the tide swept her away into the carpark, where they piled into cars and vans and onto motorbikes and drove off in a mad cavalcade, leaving members of staff standing on the front steps, wondering if there was anything they ought to do.

How far did they travel? For how long? Five minutes? Five hours? What did it matter? He was the Pied Piper, leading them over the hills and far away, to a place where the everyday world would never find them. Into a wasteland. A place of desolation and decay. Moonlight shining through empty windows, as if the ghosts that had lived there, worked there, died there, had returned for this one night. Figures huddled round a bonfire – and one upright, dancing, turning slowly round and round, casting a thin shadow two-and-a-half metres tall.

There was no talking now, no laughter. They drove on in silence, into the Country of the Damned.

Then they were there. Where? Standing beside a ruin, on a patch of waste ground, the walls above them dark and hostile. Gothic windows, like a church, or an old Victorian school – or the house of some Victorian mill-owner, before it was covered by a wave of industrial development, then left high and dry again as the factories were demolished all around.

One by one they crept inside, where the doors, fireplaces, panelling and most of the bricks of the dividing walls had all been stripped away. Through the roof Jools could see the stars, before the light inside grew too bright for her to make them out.

Banks of candles glowed all around. And there was music playing – piped music, certainly, multi-tracked, but unlike any recorded music she'd ever heard, the melody there and then gone again before you could quite fix it in your memory, and next time it came round, it was subtly changed, in a way you couldn't quite identify. The song the sirens sang, drawing you in, so that you became part of it, swaying and spinning, feet keeping time.

At the top of a crumbling flight of stairs Nick stood, a long black cloak with scarlet lining flowing from his slim shoulders. In his hand he held a tall staff, like a magician's wand. He bowed, cried, 'Welcome to my humble home!' then swung down to join the dance, never staying with one partner for long before moving on. As he came close to her, Jools said, 'Is that where you got the money? Playing Patrick at cards?'

'What money?'

'The money you spent on Mo's kids. You gave yourself away. The rocking-horse. It's all right. I won't tell.'

He smiled and took her hand. 'I'm glad you came, Juliette,' he whispered.

In a moment her other hand was taken by one of the Blues Brothers, leading a Buddhist nun. Others joined on, and soon Nick was leading a long, sinuous snake of dancers, weaving in and out and over and through the ruins, then doubling back again. Upwards he led them, along the tops of walls ten centimetres wide, no more, and over crumbling archways.

One by one the dancers' courage failed them. They dropped out and stood, still swaying in time to the music, while the rest of the snake rejoined and wound on its way. Once Jools tried to pull free, but Nick gripped her hand more tightly. 'Don't worry, Juliette. I won't let you fall.'

'What if you fall?'

'Then I shall fly!' He leaned towards her, lips brushing her cheek.

Finally he let her go, and he was dancing on alone, lithe as a cat, climbing higher and higher until there was nowhere else to go. He paused for a moment, then, with arms spread wide, stepped out into thin air.

There were gasps from the crowd below – gasps of wonder, gasps of fear – waiting for him to fall. Gradually, as their eyes made out the thin, dark line of the roof-beam against the lighter sky, the gasps turned to sighs of relief. Suddenly, at the very moment they'd decided he was going to be all right, he faltered – swayed, one foot swinging in the air – then steadied himself and, using his wand to balance with, moved forward again.

The music played on softly but no one was dancing now. Nick walked steadily on across that slender bridge, above a white sea of upturned faces. He kept his head up, feeling his way with his feet.

Halfway now: the worst was over. Then he tripped, stumbling over some hidden obstacle. He gave a little cry. People stepped out of the way as the wand plummeted down and clattered to the floor.

Above them, Nick was still struggling to keep his balance, knees bent, arms flailing, flashes of red in the darkness as the night-wind caught at his cloak. And then he fell. Fell, oh, so slowly, more like a falling leaf, twisting and tumbling down without a sound.

So little noise he made, as he hit the floor and lay still.

There was silence. Nobody moved. This was unreal.

At length Tanith stepped forward, picked up the fallen wand and prepared to lift a corner of the crumpled cloak so they could get some idea of the damage.

'Well, isn't anyone going to applaud?' Nick's voice echoed softly from somewhere behind them. He was standing at the top of the stairs, arms folded, leaning nonchalantly against the wall.

He threw back his head and laughed. 'If you could only see your faces!'

Then they did applaud, uproariously, clapping and whistling, laughing at themselves for standing there so dismayed by the sight of an empty cloak.

Nick bowed to right and left, leaped lightly down and asked, 'Did I hear a call of encore?'

'Encore!' they shouted. 'Encore!'

'By popular demand, then. Let me see . . . Not just me this time, I think. Tanith!'

Obediently she stepped forward.

'Find me two strong men,' he told her.

Quickly Tanith moved among the crowd, while the boys struck poses, showing off their muscles, offering her their biceps to feel. She picked out an Australian with corks bobbing from his hat, together with Sporting Hero, and led them forward.

One end of the room was slightly higher than the other, up a short flight of steps. Onto this stage Nick led the three of them, gathering up his cloak and wand as he went. He showed the two strong men how he wanted them to stand, facing one another, about two metres apart, fists clenched, arms outstretched – 'But not yet. Save your strength. Tanith, come here.' She came. Gently he took her face between his hands. 'Look at me, Tanith. Look into my eyes. You trust me?' His voice grew softer, caressing.

'Oh, yes,' she whispered. 'I trust you.'

'Keep looking at me. I promise you there will be no fear. No pain.'

'No fear,' she repeated drowsily. 'No pain.'

'Now close your eyes. Remember. No fear. No pain.'

He caught her as she swayed and almost fell, lifting her easily to shoulder-height. Then he nodded to the two strong men, who obediently stretched out their arms. Carefully Nick placed Tanith's rigid body between them, one supporting her shoulders, the other her feet, and folded her arms across her.

Then he took the wand and passed it underneath to show there were no hidden supports. The two strong men could have told him that: the weight on their arms was already beginning to tell.

Swiftly he took the wand – a vicious-looking thing, they could all see now, more like a spear – and wedged it between Tanith's back and the ground.

Very gently he moved away the Australian, who was holding her feet. Then Sporting Hero, who held her shoulders. There she lay, suspended in space, poised on the spear's tip.

There was a scattering of applause, swiftly hushed, as

Nick put a meaningful finger to his lips: the trick wasn't over yet. To wake her now could well be fatal.

In a breathless silence, he took her by the feet and spun her slowly round. It wasn't until she came to rest again, that a little shudder ran through her body and she dropped thirty centimetres – no more.

An answering tremor ran through the audience as they saw the red spike sticking through her chest. It was just another trick, of course – wasn't it? They looked to Nick for guidance, but, like them, he seemed to have been taken quite by surprise.

There was so little blood. She lay there, as if asleep – but, then, he'd promised there would be no pain. A trickle of blood crept down from her mouth, no more frightening, surely, than her blood-red scarf trailing to the floor. One arm, without warning, slipped and flopped lifelessly.

There was a gasp.

'Oh dear,' Nick remarked, inadequately. 'That's a pity.' With an expression of distaste, he took his cloak and draped it over the body, then held up a hand for silence. 'I'm not sure what to do now. Let me think. Anyone got a cigarette?'

Cigarettes were eagerly offered, and a lighter.

He took one, lit it and inhaled, then came to a decision. 'It seems to me – the best thing to do now is – get rid of the evidence!'

Before anyone could stop him, he stooped and touched the lighter to the end of that blood-red scarf. They stood, fascinated, as the flames licked swiftly upward, catching the cloak and setting it ablaze. It was a trick, of course. It had to be . . .

But they could see the shape of her among the flames. One of the girls screamed 'Tanith!' and went on screaming.

Someone cried out, 'That's enough!'

A boy took off his jacket and started trying to beat out the fire. A voice yelled, 'Get some water! Isn't there any water?'

Where was Nick? Jools felt the slightest movement brushing past her, light as the touch of a spider's web. She caught a glimpse in the shadows of a dark figure, backing swiftly away. Then he was gone.

Instinctively she turned and followed him, tripping over bricks and rubble, scrambling through a low window opening and dropping into a patch of weeds. Nettles stung her legs and her dress caught on a bramble. She pulled herself free and moved on, away from the house. Behind her she could hear voices shouting, girls screaming. Ahead, a shadow moved – but it was just a cat.

It had all been a trick, of course; they must have set it up between them, Nick and Tanith. A cruel, senseless, heartless trick – these were Tanith's friends, for heaven's sake, that she'd just scared half to death. Not Nick's fault: they'd wanted a Hallowe'en to remember and he'd given them one.

A couple under a streetlamp stood locked in a clinch. Not them. Her way was suddenly blocked by a rusty chain-link fence, which stretched unbroken as far as she could see to left and right. No way could Tanith have scrambled over it in that dress. She must have come too far.

Turning back towards the house she saw the lights still flickering inside. From beyond came the sound of a motor-bike driving away at speed, and car engines starting up, revved much too fast, moving away, one, then two together, then the whole fleet of them, rats leaving a sinking ship.

Hadn't anyone stopped to check – expose the whole charade?

No one, it seemed. The party was over. Inside the building, the banks of candles were burning down, guttering out one by one, making the shadows seem darker by contrast. She stood for a moment, trying to get her bearings. She wasn't alone. She could hear someone breathing softly. A foot kicked against a stone, sending it tumbling down the steps. Something brushed against her arm. Something alive. She felt a scream welling up inside her.

'It's OK, Jools,' came Joseph's voice.

'Joseph?'

'Thought you might need a lift home. Everyone else has gone.'

'You've got wheels?'

'Just the two. You'll have to ride on the cross-bar.'

'Fine Thanks. How did you know where to find me?'

'Saw you leave. Got the bike and pedalled like mad trying to keep up. Then I just cycled around until I met a couple coming away. They were well spooked! Sounds like you had quite a party.'

'Remind me to tell you about it some other time.'

'Thought I'd better make sure you got home safely.'

'Thanks.'

Home was, after all, no more than a couple of miles away, but she wouldn't have liked to have to walk it. Too many derelict sites, too many dark corners. She'd had enough excitement for one night.

Joseph dropped her outside the house and rode straight off again.

The lights were on in the kitchen. Chas sat asleep in his chair by the fire, his cigarette drooping dangerously close to his newspaper.

As Jools was taking them both gently away, he opened his eyes. 'What time is it?'

'No idea. Sorry if I'm a bit late. Joseph brought me home. You weren't worried?'

'No,' he lied. 'Can I get you anything?'

'I just want to get warm.' She crouched down close to the fire.

'Tea? Hot chocolate?'

'Chocolate would be nice. Did the Prof go out?'

'As usual.'

'His big night. Hallowe'en. They'll all be out there tonight: ghosts, witches, vampires . . .' She sat warming her hands round the mug of chocolate. 'Play something for me.'

'Past your bedtime.'

'I'm not sleepy.'

He picked up the clarinet. 'Any requests?'

She shook her head.

'How about something your mum used to sing?' He paused for a moment, almost as if he'd thought better of it, before he began to play 'Summertime'. The music spread itself around her like a warm southern afternoon, smelling of honeysuckle and roses. She felt her tangled nerves unravelling, stretching themselves like a cat in the sun. Then the tune changed slowly, subtly modulating into an old Billie Holliday number, 'Strange Fruit'. She'd learned the words when other kids were learning nursery rhymes. Taking misery and death and despair and turning them into something beautiful. That's jazz.

CHAPTER NINE

They came to the school in unmarked cars. Plain clothes. That was smart of them. If there'd been any sign of the police, on that Monday morning, quite a number of people might have turned aside at the gate and spent the day in town.

At registration, certain names were read out – Jools's among them – and they were told to go at once to the senior common room, where the Head was waiting to speak to them.

Once there – once they'd clocked the pasty-faced woman with her, who was so obviously The Law, she might as well have had it tattooed on her forehead – it was too late then to retreat.

The young guy with her, he looked OK. Round face, blond curly hair and a mouth that would turn up at the corners, no matter what: the face of a mischievous small boy.

Christopher Robin out with Nanny, thought Jools. She smiled to herself and caught his eye. No harm in exchanging smiles with a representative of The Law. Shows you've got a clear conscience.

She looked round to see who else was there, trying to pick up a clue as to why they'd been summoned. The common denominator wasn't hard to find: Hallowe'en night, Nick's party. Joseph, the one black face. Someone at the door must have been taking notes as they left the disco. One person, significantly, was missing. As if to point up the fact, the fan club sat clustered round an empty chair. Tanith was not there.

Someone got up and closed the door. Tanith wasn't coming.

Tanith was dead.

The Head broke the news as gently as she knew how. She was prepared for tears – hysteria – not for the sudden buzz of shocked excitement that ran in whispers through the room.

'He did it!'

'He really did it! Oh, my *God*!'

'He killed her!'

'And we watched him.'

'No! You saw his face – it was an accident.'

'But there was nothing – I mean, there would have been *something* left . . . Wouldn't there?'

'Surely someone—'

'Didn't anyone check, to see if she was all right?'

'Oh, shh!'

'Shh!'

'Shh!'

The policewoman might not have been able to pick out the individual words from where she sat, but she couldn't miss the overriding sense of collective guilt.

The Head waited until they were all quiet again, facing front, before she introduced the Detective Inspector and her sergeant (both names instantly forgotten), who'd like to ask them a few questions.

Jools put up her hand. 'I've got a question.' Before anyone could tell her to save it for later, she went straight on, 'Was she killed the same way as the others? *Multiple* stab-wounds? Are we talking about victim number four here?'

The DI said coldly, 'I make that three questions. Since you ask, the answer to all three is yes. Your name is—'

'Julie Cunningham.' The Head pointed to the list in front of her. 'She hasn't been with us long. You'll get on better if you call her Jools,' she added in an undertone.

Jools could feel the tension in the room easing. Tanith hadn't died by fire, nor from a stake through the heart. She could see the DI wondering what they'd thought they'd got to hide before she decided to press on, giving them the introductory spiel familiar from a dozen television series: about how important it was to trace Tanith's movements on the night she died; they must cast their minds back, try to remember every detail, anything out of the ordinary . . . (From Saturday night? thought Jools. You have to be joking!) 'We want to catch this killer before he – or she – has a chance to strike again.'

Or she? Now there was a novel thought. Unlikely, though.

The DI was continuing: 'Now, let's begin with the incident in the art room on Saturday. Would you like to tell us about it in your own words – Jools?'

'Me?' said Jools. 'Why me?'

'Why not?' asked the DI pleasantly.

'I'm not the best person. I only came in part way through.'

'From the time you came in, then.' She wasn't going to be let off the hook that easily.

'Right.' She described the scene and the course of events as matter-of-factly as she could, up to the moment when Ms Eng. Lit. came in.

'Let's get this clear,' said the DI. 'It was Nick who produced the knife?'

'He was using it for a card trick,' Jools told her firmly. 'It was Patrick who had other ideas.'

'Did anyone see or hear Patrick threaten Nick?'

The rest shook their heads. *Scumbags*.

'You could see what was in his mind,' said Jools. 'Nick was too quick for him.'

'Nevertheless, when your teacher came in, it was Nick who was threatening Patrick with the knife. I hear he actually drew blood.'

'A scratch,' said Jools. She was getting impatient

with them now. 'It was a silly little knife. You couldn't kill anyone with it. Not by stabbing wildly at them. Look: if you're looking for someone with a motive for killing Tanith on the basis of that little incident, you should be talking to Patrick. He was the one who got dumped on. He's the one with a temper.'

Though we're not looking for a motive, are we? she reminded herself. At least, not a motive that would make sense to any rational person. We're looking for a madman, with his own crazy logic.

The policewoman said icily, 'We're quite satisfied that Patrick had nothing to do with it.'

'I'll bet,' muttered Jools. Someone like Patrick was bound to have a smart lawyer on call. As it turned out, Patrick didn't need a lawyer to stand between him and a possible murder charge; he had the perfect alibi for most of Saturday night. He'd been in a police cell on charges of drunk driving, attempting to bribe a police officer and, when that didn't work, assaulting said police officer. Much more in character.

'The other person we would like to talk to is Nick Fleming,' the DI added. 'Does anyone happen to know where we might find him?'

They glanced at one another, shook their heads.

Someone murmured with a nervous giggle, 'He said *that* was where he lived.'

'That place he took us to?'

'It was a wreck! A ruin!'

When the DI asked, 'Where exactly was this?' Jools let herself relax a little more. Tanith had not been found there or they wouldn't be asking: they'd know.

The rest offered conflicting directions, until the young policeman stopped taking notes and said, 'Guv? It's OK. I know the place.'

She nodded. 'Good. Let's get on to what actually happened at this surprise party. Jools? Perhaps you'd like to continue.'

'No, thanks,' said Jools.

'Why not? You've given us a good, clear account so far.'

'Let someone else take a turn.'

There was no shortage of volunteers, as far as the early part of the evening was concerned – dancing by candlelight, under the stars, and the music, that was something wild! But somehow, in the retelling, the magic was drained out of it. As for Nick's performance on the roof-beam . . .

'We thought he'd fallen.'

'We really did.'

'It was dead funny, when you think about it, the way he managed to slip round behind us.'

'All of us looking the wrong way!'

'So simple!'

So simple. She'd like to see one of them pull off the same trick.

As the rest of the story unfolded, they grew more hesitant, unsure what was real and what was unreal. Sporting Hero and Oz (he was stuck with that nickname now) affirmed that they'd been holding the full weight of Tanith's body, until the spear was in place – but the spear couldn't have supported her, could it? Not without . . . what happened – or seemed to happen. And then the fire!

There was fear in the air now, rekindling their last sight of Tanith, flames licking upward around her seemingly lifeless body.

On the three adults' faces distaste mingled with disbelief.

'And then?' the DI prompted.

They looked at one another. A voice said lamely, 'Then we all went home.'

'What about Tanith?'

'What about her?'

'Didn't anyone think to check whether she was all right? Where was she?'

They shook their heads, ashamed, embarrassed.

'With Nick, I suppose.'

'I suppose he took her home.'

They looked at one another for confirmation.

Jools said clearly, 'She wasn't with Nick. Nick was with me. He took me home.'

She saw Joseph half turn his head towards her, but he didn't contradict her.

She kept her face expressionless while she sent up a quick prayer that they wouldn't ask her what kind of car Nick drove . . .

'What time was it when you got home?'

She shook her head. 'Sorry. No idea. After midnight. My dad was up, but he asked me the time and I didn't know.' After midnight still left several hours in which Nick could have met up with Tanith afterwards, if he'd wanted to. 'They weren't an item,' said Jools. 'Nick and Tanith. They just got together to cook up this Hallowe'en entertainment.'

'With what purpose?'

'Fun, I suppose.'

'Fun,' repeated the DI. 'It wasn't really very funny, was it?'

Jools explained patiently, 'It was just an illusion. Tanith had to be in on it. She was the reason most of us were there in the first place. Come on! It was a trick. A variation on the old Lady Vanishes routine. There was no need for everyone to freak out, just because he didn't put Humpty Dumpty back together again.'

The DI was giving her a hard stare. 'And are *you* an item? You and Nick?'

'No way!' Caught off-guard, Jools felt herself blushing. 'No, we're just friends.' She appealed to the Head, 'You did say that none of the girls were to walk home alone? He was just making sure I got home safely. Was that what happened to Tanith? Was she attacked on the way home?'

The three grown-ups looked at one another. 'She

seems to have reached home safely,' the DI said quietly. 'There was no sign of a break-in. We think she opened the door herself to her attacker, which means it was almost certainly someone she knew.'

A voice from the back asked tremulously, 'What about her parents? Where were they?'

'Her parents were away for the weekend.'

Poor Tanith. Jools had never expected to find herself thinking that. Poor Tanith, alone in the house with a killer. No one to hear her scream. Nowhere to run.

The young sergeant was putting his notebook away. The DI was gathering up her things. 'If no one has any further questions,' she said, 'I'll just repeat what I said at the beginning. Any piece of information, no matter how trivial it seems to you, is worth mentioning. If you'd rather speak to one of us in confidence, you can call this number.' She pinned a card to the notice-board. After a bit of hesitation – no one wanting to show too much interest – they gathered round to jot the number down on odd scraps of paper, just to show willing.

Then they were free to go.

As Jools went out, Joseph gave her a look that managed to be hurt, puzzled and angry all at the same time.

Jools didn't go near him until she was sure she was out of sight of Plod's prying eyes. 'Joseph!'

He didn't look at her. 'What was that about?' he muttered, walking on quickly, so that she had to give a hop and a skip every few steps to keep up.

'They're trying to put Nick in the frame for Tanith's murder. That's stupid. You think he'd draw attention to the two of them like that, then take her off and kill her? He'd have to be insane!'

'Whoever killed those girls is insane.'

Jools said firmly, 'It wasn't Nick. The police are just looking for someone to pull in, so they can tell the press they've got a suspect.'

'So what? When they find they can't match him up with the other murders, they'll let him go again.'

'What if he can't prove he was somewhere else when the other murders happened? "I was home in bed, alone." What sort of alibi is that? There'll be no way of proving his innocence unless there's another murder while he's under arrest. Great!'

'I still don't like it. Chas is a mate. I don't like lying to a mate.'

'You don't have to lie to Chas. Just to the police, maybe, if you have to. Look, all I'm saying is, if Chas asks, you brought me home; if Plod asks, you didn't. Nick's a mate, too. You look after your mates. That's all I'm trying to do.'

She hadn't lied to Chas and yet that lie lay between them like a sleeping dragon. She hadn't lied to Chas, but what if the police came to the house to check with him on the time that she'd arrived home and happened to ask him who'd brought her?

But they didn't. At least, he didn't say they had. He said, 'That was a terrible thing that happened to your friend.'

'She wasn't my friend,' said Jools.

'Do you want to talk about it?'

'No. No, thanks.' She was afraid of what she might blurt out. Because normally she always told him everything.

'Any time you're ready.' She'd hurt his feelings.

*　　*　　*

At school, the week dragged on towards the half-term break.

The young sociology teacher was off on sick leave. He blamed himself for what had happened.

Ms Eng. Lit. abandoned any attempt to teach *Othello*, with its memories of Tanith aka Desdemona pleading for her life. Instead she screened a video of *Much Ado About Nothing*, suggesting they might like to consider the villain in that, Don John, as an early sketch for Iago. Evil for its own sake. More a case of post-traumatic stress, Jools decided; the effect of fighting in whatever war it was they'd just got back from. Nowadays he'd be offered counselling, before he got the chance to wreck other people's lives. There was counselling on offer, in spades, for Tanith's friends and classmates, but few takers, even among the fan club. People kept bursting into tears for no special reason, but it wasn't grief. It was more relief, that death had come so close and passed them by. They didn't want counsellors, they wanted Tanith – Tanith would have shown them how to behave. They were angry with her for leaving them in the lurch.

Paparazzi hovered round the school gates until

the Head shooed them away. Then they lurked at a distance, like predatory cats, ready to leap at any tear-stained face. Journos, notebook in hand, demanded, 'Were you a friend of hers, love? How do you feel?'

'Devastated, of course,' answered Jools, annoyed with herself for not having seen this one lurking behind the phone box up ahead.

'You're devastated?' He made a note.

'No, not really. But I think that's the word you're looking for.'

She walked on, wondering why people were so interested in violent death — as long as it wasn't their own.

Even Brenda — who'd been blanking her completely since she came out from buying her lottery tickets and found Jools teaching Albie junior to blow raspberries — Brenda actually crossed the street to speak to her. 'Hallo, Jools.'

'Hallo,' said Jools. 'Hallo, young Albie.'

The baby blew a raspberry.

'I heard the news,' said Brenda. 'About your friend. It's terrible.'

'I'm devastated,' said Jools.

'Mm. Yes. I expect you are. Don't worry, love, they'll catch him.'

'Him?' Jools stonewalled.

'Stands to reason, doesn't it? Must be a man. They know who they're looking for. It's always the same description, isn't it? In the paper. A bit like that fella I saw you with.'

Jools gave her a blank stare.

'Thin, clean-shaven, with long, dark hair, aged about twenty, snappy dresser,' Brenda prompted.

'Not much to go on, is it?' said Jools. 'If he's got anything to hide, he'll have cut his hair by now, grown a beard and started buying his clothes from Oxfam.'

'Yes.' Brenda agreed, but slowly. She was reluctant to let the idea go: my friend, the friend of a serial killer. 'Well, must press on!' said Brenda brightly. 'Goodbye, Jools.'

'Bye,' said Jools.

CHAPTER TEN

Tuesday limped by, and Wednesday, then Thursday. On the Friday, as they turned into Park Road on the way home from school – Joseph always walked her home now, it was a habit they'd got into – Jools spotted a little Morris Traveller parked outside the house. The back was piled high with clothes, cushions, pots and pans and bric-à-brac, as if the owner had been out collecting for a jumble sale. In the front, a little brown figure sat hunched behind the steering wheel, like a bird with its feathers fluffed up against the cold.

'Lady Rachel!' Jools knocked on the window, then stepped smartly back as the driver's door shot open and the dumpy figure hurtled towards her and fastened itself round her waist. 'Lady Rachel!' It was a bit like hugging a cushion: somewhere under the layers of clothes there must be a body.

How long was it since they'd last seen one another? Nearly two years? After the first rush of excitement, they'd pick up the threads as if that gap had never been, until, in a day, a week, a month, one of them decided it was time to move on. That was the way it was with most people Jools knew – correction: with everyone, bar Chas.

Once her feet were on solid ground again, Lady Rachel straightened her clothes and settled her straw hat more firmly on her head. 'Jools! You're a sight for sore eyes!'

'Don't cry, then.' Jools fumbled for a handkerchief. 'What's the matter?'

'I thought I'd never find you.' She sniffed, took the proffered handkerchief, then wiped her nose on her sleeve.

'You came looking for us? Why?'

'Sam tells me I've got to find you, pretty damn quick. He's got his reasons, but he won't tell me, oh no! I'm just his poor old mother, got to go where he tells me. So I'm driving round and round, asking has anyone seen a muso and his little girl. Sam says, "But, little mother, she's a big girl now, you silly old woman." I forgot.' She struck her forehead with the heel of her hand. 'Losing my marbles. Sam gets so cross. Sometimes, weeks at a time, he won't speak to me at all.' She seemed about to cry again. Then, seeing Joseph, she perked up. 'This your young man?'

Jools said, 'This is Joseph. Joseph, meet Lady Rachel.'

Lady Rachel dropped a curtsy and Joseph grinned. 'I never met a real lady before.'

'You still ain't,' said Lady Rachel equably. 'They calls me that out of respect, because I got the Sight. Hot line to the Other Side – an' I don't mean Moscow! My baby, Sam. He died, you know . . .' Her voice trailed away, remembering.

You had to hand it to Joseph: he didn't bat an eyelid. 'My nan does a bit of that,' he said, 'fortune-telling, with the cards.'

'Cards!' she exclaimed. 'This old woman, she don't need no cards. Your face is your fortune, Joseph. Come on, now, give me a kiss, and I'll tell you your fortune. Gypsy women say cross my palm with silver, but I tell you straight, a young man's kiss to an old woman, that's worth more than silver.'

Laughing, Joseph bent and kissed her.

'Ooooh!' Lady Rachel mimed near to swooning. 'You have witchcraft in your lips, Joseph! Joseph, let's see. Joseph, I see you in a coat of many colours, like in the Bible – yes? Joseph, filling the world with music! True?'

Joseph gave Jools a surprised look.

Jools shrugged. 'I didn't tell her.'

Lady Rachel gave a gleeful chuckle. 'No! She didn't tell me: I seed for myself you busking at the park gates yesterday, when I was driving round and round. Lordy,' she nudged Jools, 'these gawjos is easy to fool!' Then she was solemn again. 'Poor Joseph! So unlucky in love!' She shook her head. 'You ain't the one. Sam says he's got to talk to your young man, Jools, but this ain't the one. Pity – he's got good teeth. Bad teeth is bad temper. Good teeth don't mean the reverse, o' course,' she added reflectively.

'Have you seen Chas yet?' asked Jools, seizing her chance to cut in, since she didn't want to be standing here for another hour or more.

'I've seen him,' answered Lady Rachel.

167

'Then why are you still sitting out here? Won't you come in? Have a cup of tea?'

Lady Rachel looked up at the house. 'Chas asked me that already. Sam says to wait for you outside. Sam don't like this place. Bad vibes. What's he doin'?' she demanded. 'That old man up there, staring at us?'

Glancing up, Jools saw the Professor standing motionless at the front bedroom window. She gave a cheery wave, trying to embarrass him into moving away. Some hopes!

'Take no notice,' said Jools. 'You don't have to meet him.'

But Lady Rachel clamped herself onto Joseph's arm. 'You go in and talk to your dad,' she told Jools. 'Joseph will show me around.'

Joseph glanced down at the little figure looking trustingly up at him. 'It's OK, Jools,' he said. 'No problem. I'll look after her. See you later, eh? Down the Spotted Cow. Come on, Lady Rachel. Is Sam coming with us? Come along, then, Sam. Mind how you cross the road.'

Jools stood looking after them until they reached the park. As she turned away, she almost bumped into the Professor coming out of the front door. She moved to one side to let him past, but he stood blocking the steps.

'I have been watching you,' he said.

'I noticed.'

'But I cannot be watching you all the time. You do not see the danger.'

She said nothing, just waited for him to shift.

'You still wear the cross I gave you? Let me see.'

She showed him.

He seemed only partly satisfied: 'You must be careful who you are seen with,' he told her solemnly, 'who you are talking to.'

'Lady Rachel's an old friend. She can leave the car there for a bit, can't she? It is a public highway.'

He only sighed and shook his head and walked past her down the steps, out into the night.

Down in the kitchen, she said to Chas, 'Guess who I've seen.'

'Lady Rachel?'

'Why didn't you invite her in?'

'I did.' He shrugged. 'She wouldn't come.'

'Sam's orders, I suppose.'

'I took her out a cup of tea and a custard cream. We chatted for a bit. She insisted on waiting for you out there.'

'Sam said. She's getting worse. Time was when Sam was just sort of in the background. Now it seems she can't make a move unless Sam says – like some stupid party game! Why can't he leave her alone?'

'Imagine he did. What would she do then?'

'She might get herself a life. She can't be that old.'

'No older than me.'

'Woh! No kidding! She looks ancient.'

'Comes of living rough in all weathers.' He smiled, remembering. 'When she's not actually there, in front of me, I always think of her as she used to be, before Sam died. Sunshine in her hair and roses in her cheeks. Where is she now?'

'Joseph's looking after her.'

'Joseph?'

'He took her in his stride, Baby Sam and all.'

'He's a good lad.'

She chuckled. 'The only thing that fazed him was when she asked if he was my young man.'

'You could do worse.'

'Hm! That's about what I'd say about you and Josie.'

'You mean I could do better?'

'I mean, I don't need a mother, Chas. If Josie's good for you, for a while, that's fine by me.'

Slowly he nodded, held out his arms and folded them round her, rubbing his cheek against her hair. 'Just you and me, eh, Julie?'

When they got to the Spotted Cow that evening, Lady Rachel was already in residence, tucking into her second helping of apple pie with custard *and* ice cream, having already done justice to Josie's home-made soup, followed by roast beef with all the trimmings.

'You'll be about ready for another pint, then?' said Chas, picking up her empty glass. 'Bitter?'

'Best bitter!' instructed Lady Rachel, with an unladylike belch.

'Best bitter, please, Josie. There go tomorrow night's wages,' he added ruefully, as Lady Rachel pushed aside her pudding plate and reached for the cheese and biscuits.

'Don't be daft,' said Josie. 'If I can't spare a bite to eat for a friend of yours, though where she puts it all . . .'

'Most of the time she doesn't get enough to keep a sparrow alive.'

'Well, just so long as she doesn't go spreading it around that this is the place to come for a free feed. Anyway, it was well worth the price of the meal to hear all about you.'

'Lies. All lies.'

'Oh, I hope not! I like a man with a past.'

In the back room someone was playing the piano. 'Joseph?' asked Chas.

Josie nodded. 'They've been at it now for nearly an hour.'

He frowned, listening. 'Who's that on the drums? Albie?'

The question was answered in the negative by the arrival of Albie himself, breezing in through the street door.

'Nice timing,' said Chas. 'I was just getting them in.'

'Cheers, mate. Mine's a pint.'

'Better see what the boys in the back room will have.' Chas left some money on the bar and carried over a pint of bitter, and a bitter lemon for Jools, to Lady Rachel's table.

Lady Rachel stabbed her cheese-knife in Jools's direction. 'You're growin' out of that jacket. Soon be needing new.'

Jools smiled. 'Will you make me one? You and Sam?'

Lady Rachel listened carefully for a moment. 'Sam says he ain't sure if we'll be here. Best if you choose for yourself this time.'

Jools nodded, then she sat listening to the music. The drums were setting the pace, nudging the piano-player into sudden changes of tempo, style, mood, giving him the confidence to try out fresh flights of fancy, but always there ahead of him, ready to catch him if he fell and lift him up to try again. Someone was giving Joseph a thorough musical work-out.

Albie came back with a half-full mug. 'Just a top-up for Joseph,' he told Josie. 'Lager shandy. Says he's got to keep a clear head.' He seemed uneasy, fingers

173

tapping on the bar in time with the drums. 'Good drums, yeah?'

Chas nodded.

'You coming through?'

'In a minute.'

'When you're ready.' Albie vanished into the back room again. Soon afterwards, the piano fell silent – Joseph taking some well-earned refreshment – but the drums played on.

Lady Rachel sat back, legs stretched out, looking round at the mirrored walls. 'This is a good place,' she decided. 'Good grub. I could die happy, after a meal like that.'

Behind the bar, Josie quietly glowed with pleasure at the compliment.

Chas leaned on the counter, staring at the drink in his glass.

The beat of the drums went on and on, insistent, elusive. No one, apart from Jools, seemed to be paying any attention. Jungle drums, carrying a message just for her, wakening echoes locked deep in her memory, from a time even before she was born. Siren music, drawing her closer.

As she stood up, the figures in the mirrors broke into a silent dance, weaving and turning, joining and parting, shepherding her onwards.

The drummer was Nick. He sat, head bent, face hidden by a soft curtain of hair, lost in the Devil's music as he played. Then he looked up and smiled. There was a quickening in the beat, which matched the quickening of her pulse as she smiled back.

Joseph sat by the piano, engrossed in the rhythm, any reservations about Nick plainly forgotten. Why should that surprise her? Nick could charm the birds from the trees or the paper off the walls if he set his mind to it.

She didn't notice that Chas had followed her into the room, until Nick, looking past her, said, 'Hi, Chas.' He went on playing without missing a beat, went on smiling, but his eyes were suddenly ice-cold.

Albie, too, was looking in their direction. Albie, immediately disclaiming all responsibility, 'Not my idea, Chas. I just found him here.'

'Come to join us?' said Nick to Chas. 'Make up a foursome? Bring back a few memories?'

Albie, still hoping for a quiet life, urged, 'Give the

lad a chance, eh, Chas? You heard him from out there. You said he was good.'

With an effort, Chas said, 'I told you to get him a drink.'

Nick, still smiling, still playing, punctuating the words with sudden flourishes, answered, 'Thanks, but no thanks. I don't drink. It doesn't agree with me. Runs in the family. Like father, like son. Like mother, like daughter.' He gestured towards Jools. 'No doubt at all who her mother was. Uncanny, isn't it? Déjà vu.'

Chas flashed a glance from Jools to Nick and back again, then snapped at Albie, 'OK. He's had his chance. Now get rid of him!'

Suddenly Jools felt Chas's arm around her, half dragging, half pushing her across the room. 'I want a word with you, young lady,' he said.

'What, now?' she protested, as he bundled her through the kitchen door. Josie looked up from piling the dirty dishes in the sink. 'What's up, love? You look as if you'd seen a ghost.'

Chas said, 'Can you give us a few minutes alone, please, Josie?'

She gave a brief glance from one to the other.

'Of course. I'll finish this later.' She wiped her hands quickly, then left them to it.

'Well?' demanded Jools.

Chas took a deep breath. 'How long have you known him?'

She acted injured innocence. 'Who? Nick? Not long. We haven't been here long.'

'From now on, stay away from him.'

'Would you mind telling me why?'

'Because I say so. He's bad news, Jools.'

'How can you say that? You don't even know him!'

'I know – the type.'

'The type!' she repeated. 'Is that all? Is that really all? Look at me, Chas! Talk to me! Like mother, like daughter, he said. It's something to do with my mother, isn't it?'

He looked at her, guilty as hell. 'What's he been saying to you?'

'Only that I should ask you for the truth about my mother. That's fair enough, isn't it? So, come on, Chas. I'm waiting.'

There was a long silence. 'Not here,' he said at

last. 'Not now. Just promise me – for the moment – you'll keep away from him.'

'You have to give me a reason, Chas.'

'Because I'm telling you!'

She shook her head. 'Not good enough. I'm sixteen, Chas. I don't have to do as you say. I may not be able to buy myself a drink from the bar or drive a car, but I can choose my own friends – have sex – walk out and never come back, if I want.' Why did she have to add that? She could have bitten her tongue out the moment after, at the stricken look on his face. His voice, when he spoke again, was barely more than a whisper. 'Go, then.'

He didn't mean it. He thought that if he said that she'd climb down off her high horse. She might have done, if he hadn't added bitterly, 'I thought I'd brought you up to have better taste!' Instead she called his bluff, turned on her heel and stalked out of the room.

If Chas wouldn't tell her anything, then Nick would.

But Nick was no longer there. She found Albie alone in the back room with Samantha.

'What's up with Chas?' asked Albie. He shook his

head, bewildered. 'It's not like him. I mean, it's all of sixteen years! Can't blame the kid for what his old man did.'

'What did he do, Albie?'

He gave her a long, mournful look, then turned away, confiding to Samantha, 'We never knew the whole story, did we?'

'Where's Nick now?'

He gestured towards the bar. But the bar was empty, apart from Joseph. Lady Rachel had gone too. She'd scarcely touched her drink. In the mirrors the dance was over. Shadowy figures whispered silently among themselves.

'What happened to Lady Rachel?' Jools asked Joseph.

'Went out just now with Nick. Do they know each other?'

'I don't think so. Why?'

'I just got the impression it was him she really came to see. Hey! He's OK, is Nick. Ace drummer. Where you going, Jools?'

But the door was already swinging to behind her. Why was she suddenly so afraid?

*   *   *

Outside in the dark, she looked to left and right. A hundred metres down the street, lamplight shone briefly on a couple moving slowly away, striking a flash of flame in the man's dark hair as he bent towards the dumpy little woman by his side. They looked so comfortable together that, instead of running to catch up, Jools followed at a distance. He had his arm round her, like a lover. She rested her head against him as they walked in step towards Rats' Alley.

From the footbridge Jools watched them as they came out into the space where the four pathways met. There they sat down, looking solemnly at one another. Just for a moment, Nick glanced upward, towards the footbridge and Jools knew he'd seen her standing there. Then he turned back to Lady Rachel and, gently brushing aside the grey-streaked hair, he bent his head and sank his teeth into her neck.

She didn't struggle. Anyone passing by would have taken them for a courting couple, nothing more sinister than that. But Jools had seen. She knew. She tried to cry out, but the words caught in her throat.

Then she was clattering down the iron steps,

running along the street, flinging herself headlong into the darkness, with the sound of footsteps and her own breathing echoing off the tunnel walls, bursting into the light again. At last she found her voice. 'Lady Rachel!'

Nick lifted his head to tell her gently, 'She can't hear you.'

From behind him came Lady Rachel's voice, fractious as a sleepy child: 'Course I can hear her! It's OK, Jools. This is what I came for. Sam promised he would help us, your young man. Don't be sad. This way is best.'

Nick smoothed her hair and laid her down gently on the bench, then bent his head again.

Jools stood frozen in horrified fascination. What she was seeing was too monstrous to believe. A part of her half expected them both to sit up at any minute and laugh at her for taking it so seriously. Deep down she knew that this was not another Hallowe'en party trick. And still she couldn't make a move to stop him. And then it was too late.

He sat up and, taking a tissue from his pocket, dabbed at the corners of his mouth. He beckoned her closer. 'Come here, Juliette. Come and look. See how peaceful she is.'

'You killed her.' She said it out loud, mainly to convince herself. She couldn't believe it, that he could sit there so calmly.

'You heard what she said: it was the best thing for both of them.' He seemed half in a dream. 'Always that sweet taste of heaven,' he said softly. Carefully he arranged the body so that it looked as if Lady Rachel was sleeping. Later – perhaps not till morning – someone would try, unsuccessfully, to move her on. Just another bag lady who hadn't made it through the night, like the old wino from the park. Was this how he'd died, too? And the murdered girls . . .

'What about the others?' She began backing away from him. 'They weren't so easy to persuade, were they? That's why you made such a mess of it!'

'Juliette . . .' He was turning towards her.

'Keep away from me!' Then she was running again, running for her life, through the darkness and out into the light. Too late she realised she'd picked the wrong tunnel. Instead of taking the way back to the pub, she'd come out on the other side of the main road.

Metal barriers prevented her from crossing, even if she felt like taking her chance in among the fast-moving traffic. There was a set of lights further down where she could cross, but she hadn't taken more than a dozen steps towards them when she looked up and saw Nick standing, hands in pockets, waiting for her. Quickly she turned right into the main shopping centre. The thing was to keep where there were lights and people. The bigger shops were closed by now. She scanned the smaller ones as she hurried past – a newsagent's, an off-licence, a video rental – but there was no place to hide. She half ran the length of the arcade and risked a quick glance behind her: had she lost him? It seemed as if she had. She ducked into the Italian restaurant on the corner and stood trying to watch both windows at once, until a waiter began to usher her to a table. She hadn't even got the price of a coffee, so she left, by the street door.

No sign of him.

She was closer to home now than she was to the Spotted Cow. What was it the Prof had said about her room? Her own place, where no one could enter uninvited. One last dash, then, through the park, that was the best way. There would still be people about. She crossed the road and broke into a jog as she entered the park.

Night-wind blowing through her hair, gravel crunching underfoot and the sound of a fountain splashing in the distance. The autumn smell of bonfires and fallen leaves. She began to feel calmer. Dark bushes, glistening damp, rising higher and higher on either side and a figure silently running beside her.

Without breaking step she turned her head and saw Nick smiling back at her. She started to run faster, but he easily outpaced her. A little way ahead he turned and stopped.

Jools stopped too: she had no choice unless she wanted to cannon straight into him. She looked around. There wasn't another soul in sight. A thicket of rhododendrons hemmed her in, with roots and branches waiting to snag and trip her. She wouldn't get five metres, if she went that way.

He was moving towards her now.

'That's close enough!' she cried, fumbling for the silver cross at her throat. Then she remembered that he'd touched the cross – even admired it. So much for superstition. There was no protection. None at all. Nowhere was safe.

'Juliette . . .'

'I'm not your Juliette. I'm Jools. Now get away from me!'

He stopped and, spreading his hands wide, protested gently, 'I won't hurt you, Jools. If you held a knife to my throat or levelled a stake at my heart, I still wouldn't lift a finger to hurt you. Not you.'

'No?' She was not convinced. 'What's special about me?'

'I didn't kill those girls, Jools.'

She wanted to believe him – oh, how she wanted to believe!

'Convince me.'

He answered simply, 'It's not in my nature. You've seen how I kill: no fear, no pain.' He shook his head and sighed. 'To waste so much good young blood! That *is* what I call a crime! I'm sorry: that remark was in very bad taste.' He was close to her now, reaching out, fingers stroking her hair. 'You don't really believe I killed them.' His eyes were sad, reproachful.

She willed herself to stay calm. He'd said he wouldn't hurt her: if he meant to hurt her, she'd be dead by now. 'You did know them. All of them.'

He nodded. 'Better than you will ever know another human being.'

'You drank their blood.'

'It's what I do,' he answered simply. 'I'm a vampire.'

'Mine too? Did you drink my blood, too?'

'Oh, yes.' Looking into his beautiful eyes, her mind went back to that evening by the fire and a scratch she'd discovered next morning on the inside of her elbow that she couldn't account for. She remembered feeling a bit drowsy, a bit dizzy. Meanwhile he was there, inside her head, sharing her memories, thoughts, hopes, fears.

'You might have asked first!' she protested.

His eyes were sparkling like sunlight on the water. 'Oh, Juliette, I love it when you make me laugh!'

She said awkwardly, 'I ought to go. Chas'll be wondering where I am.'

But as she turned away, he caught her wrist, not tightly enough to hurt, only to hold her fast. 'Don't you want to hear the rest of my story?' he asked. He smiled engagingly. 'We left our poor vampire in a very sad state. Alone. And in hell, for ever.'

Reluctantly, but curious, she asked, 'What happened to him, then?'

Nick said softly, 'He fell in love. After two hundred and fifty years, he allowed himself to fall in love with a mortal woman.' Still holding her by the left hand, he slid his right arm round her waist, like a dancing partner, swaying in time to a song only he could hear. Softly he went on, 'It was her voice that snared him. She sang with the voice of an angel, so that he was almost ready to believe he wasn't quite shut out from heaven, after all. Then it occurred to him that sharing a human life, from youth to old age, was something he'd never done. That was all he wanted: to share a human life. To drink her blood from time to time, so as to know each new experience with her. In return, he would have given her the world!

'But there was another man who wanted her too. He gave her the one thing a vampire could never give her. A baby. He gave her you, Jools. So I lost her. Then she died. End of story. Everyone dies,' he added plaintively, 'except me. Be quiet now! There's someone coming.'

She felt his body close against her, quite still, shielding her, as the unseen passer-by went on his way without a pause. How did they look to him? A single, darker shadow among shadows, no movement, no scent. As the footsteps died away, she felt his lips against hers.

'Your lips are warm,' she murmured in surprise.

'Are they? Must be the blood.'

'Lady Rachel's blood.' She drew away from him.

'She came to me for help. If you had read her mind, as I did, you would understand there was no hope there, none at all.'

'There's always hope,' protested Jools. 'Tomorrow – the next day – something might happen, something quite unexpected . . .'

He said sadly, 'She would never have let him go, Jools. You have to know when to let go. If Chas had let your mother go, she might still be alive today.'

'Oh, that's cruel!'

He wrapped his arms round her again. 'I'm sorry,'

he murmured. 'Even if I thought it, it was wrong to say it.'

'Why did you come back?' she asked miserably. 'We were fine as we were.'

He reflected for a moment. 'Curiosity, at first. To see how you were getting on. After I'd met you, I wanted you to understand me – to like me. That's why I told you the story of my life. Then, with the first taste of your blood, I knew I wanted you. That's why I stayed. In spite of the danger, I had to stay.'

She drew her head back to look at him. 'Danger? What danger?'

'Whoever killed those girls, it's me he's really after.'

'Who?'

'Someone who hates me.'

'Killing them, to put the blame on you? That's sick!'

He shook his head. 'There's more to it than that, I think. Some nights I can sense him, following me, but afraid to come too close. That morning, when I left Tanith, I should have warned her not to open the door after I'd gone.'

'So you were with her!'

'She was alone and nervous: what else could I do but stay? I would have done the same for you.'

'Or any other girl, I suppose?'

'I do believe you're jealous, Jools!' He chuckled.

'Of Tanith? Not any more.' She rested her head against him. 'I never believed you killed her. I lied for you. I told the police you were with me that night.'

'You wish!' he teased. 'It's not the police I'm afraid of. Except that if they lock me up, there'll be no one to protect you. Even standing here with you, now, I may be putting you in danger. What am I to do, Jools? Perhaps I should simply go away.' He stepped back, as if preparing to leave now, this minute. 'Then the killings would stop. But I don't want to leave you.' The sadness in his eyes! 'If I really cared for you, Juliette, then I'd go.'

'Don't go!' she begged him. 'Please, don't go.'

'You're right,' he said slowly. 'I can't be certain if I left that you'd be completely safe.' Suddenly a brilliant idea seemed to strike him. 'Come with me. Now! Tonight! Then we'll both be safe. And I can show you the world, Juliette! Ask me for anything! Whatever you want to do . . . Wherever you want to go . . . Where shall we go first? Name anywhere! The place where you'd like to go most in all the world!'

She laughed. 'I don't know! I can't think! New Orleans – Mardi Gras.'

'That's months away. How shall we fill in the time till then? Shall I show you the Pyramids by moonlight? Shall we take the golden road to Samarkand? The rainforest – you must see the rainforest before it's gone for ever! I'll call the dolphins to swim with you in warm seas off some deserted coral island. And afterwards, we'll make love under the stars – if that's what you want. I only want what you want. I want to see it through your eyes.'

'Stop it, Nick!' She put her hands to her head, running her fingers through her hair. Why couldn't he have kept it simple? Why not just stop at 'Come with me'? 'I need time to think.'

'Don't take too long. Each day I spend here now is dangerous for both of us. Don't look so worried. I won't let anyone hurt you. Think of it as a game! Come on, I'll take you home.'

Outside the house in Park Road, he stopped and folded his arms around her. 'The thrill of the hunt!' he said softly, looking up at the dark walls. 'There's nothing like it for sharpening the senses. The question now is: which one is the hunted and which the hunter?'

She watched him go, sauntering along the dark, empty street, whistling softly, but wary, as if he expected someone to follow, but no one did, as far as she could see.

CHAPTER ELEVEN

Josie had brought Chas home and stayed to keep him company, no chatter, no fuss. She'd made herself a cup of tea and was sitting at the table, drinking it, when Jools came in. Chas was hunched in the armchair, staring moodily into the fire, nursing a mug of what looked like hot milk but gave off a whiff of something stronger.

'Here she is now!' exclaimed Josie, a bit too brightly. 'Didn't I tell you she'd find her own way home soon enough? Cup of tea, love? It's not long made.'

Jools nodded. 'Yes, please.'

Josie poured the tea, then picked up her coat. 'Well, I must be off. I left Albie looking after the bar, but if the lager goes, I don't want him trying to put on a new barrel all by himself. No need to worry about the Prof,' she told Jools. 'I've put a Thermos of soup up there for when he comes in, and a bit of game pie and salad.' She gave Chas a quick kiss. 'I should get off to bed, lover, soon as you can. Things'll look better in the morning.'

She beckoned Jools after her as she went out of the door. Jools pulled it to behind them. Josie whispered, 'If he doesn't want to tell me what's bothering him, love, then I don't want to know. But try and get him to talk to you. It does no good, bottling things up.' She shook her head, as if she knew from experience. 'No good at all.'

'Thanks, Josie.'

'My pleasure.' Josie leaned forward and kissed her on the cheek. 'I'll see myself out. You go and look after him.'

She was OK, was Josie.

'What was all that about?' asked Chas.

'Just girl talk. She's worried about you.'

He pulled a face. 'Pour me a cup of tea, will you? I can't drink this. You'd think a woman who runs a pub would have more respect for good booze.'

She took the cup of whisky and milk and poured

it down the sink. 'Josie said we ought to talk. Talk to me, Chas.' It was only fair to hear Chas's side of the story. Without prejudice. Without telling him what Nick had told her.

'What about?'

'You know what about. What was all that? Between you and Nick.'

He was looking around him, avoiding meeting her eyes. 'I need a smoke.'

She passed him the tin. 'Here. Now tell me.'

He glanced at her briefly, then focused all his attention on rolling himself a cigarette. At last he said, 'It was as if I walked through that door and found myself back sixteen – seventeen years ago. I could see it all happening again.' He ran his tongue along the paper. 'The dead spit of his father! The way he looked at you! So hungry! So sure of himself.' He bent down to get a light from the fire. 'He wanted her. Wanted her the way a child wants something: I want – I get! Wouldn't take no for answer. At first – I don't know – he had a certain charm, I suppose. Later, when she was expecting you – and after . . . She got so ill. Anaemic. Anorexic. Afraid of her own shadow.' He shook his head. 'If it had been drugs, I'd have known how to get help. But it was her mind not her body he was poisoning, until she didn't have a thought in her head to call her own and he was putting the craziest ideas in their place.'

'What kind of ideas?'

'Like that pose you saw this evening – never accepting a drink; always saying he had to be home before daylight; talking about the battle of Culloden, the French Revolution, as if he'd been there, done that . . . That he taught Van Gogh how to look at the stars and gave Bram Stoker the idea for *Dracula*. With the rest of us – compared to some of the weirdos we knew – he didn't score particularly high. She was an innocent. He really had her believing all that garbage! That he was a vampire, two hundred years old; that he'd been drinking her blood . . . Recently, talking to the Prof – he lost his wife, you know?'

She nodded. 'I know.'

'Of course, there are no such things as vampires! But I got to thinking about it all again. He – Nick Fleming – the one I knew – he was a kind of vampire. In a way. Draining the life out of her. The energy.

That's what she meant when she said he was drinking her blood. There are people like that. That's what I meant when I said I know the type.'

'What happened to her? How did she die?'

It seemed like an age before he answered, deliberately, 'She drove the car into a brick wall. The coroner was kind enough to say it was an accident.'

'Oh,' was all she said, and she breathed again. Not Nick, she thought. All she could feel was relief that it hadn't been Nick who'd killed her, the same way he'd killed Lady Rachel.

'Your grandma said it was my fault she died. Perhaps, in a way, it was. Perhaps if I'd let her go with him – but I'd never have let her take you!'

She couldn't think of anything to say. *It wasn't Nick*. Nick was no more to blame than Chas.

'Why didn't you tell me this before?' she asked him.

He said quietly, 'To have a mother who went mad and died the way she did – that's not an easy thing for a child to live with. Then, as time went on, it was just easier to say nothing.'

Not mad, Chas. Not mad. It was the truth she told you.

'Then he sends his son – after sixteen years! Can he really still hate me that much? Sending his son to get at me through you?'

Not his son, Chas. How could she tell him that?

So they sat in their separate silences, further apart than ever, until at length he stood up. 'I'm tired, Jools. I'm going to bed.'

'OK,' she said absently. 'Don't smoke in bed. I don't want to have throw a bucket of water over you.'

'No.' He forced a smile and, dutifully pinching out his cigarette, left it in the ashtray. 'Night.'

'Night, Chas. Love you.'

'Yes.'

She sat for a long while, staring into the fire, thinking about how one secret had been replaced by another. How could she say to Chas: 'Mum wasn't mad. This is the same Nick Fleming that she knew. He is a vampire, nearly three hundred years old. He's drunk my blood, too and – so what? – I feel fine.' Chas would think *she* was mad.

He is a vampire and I've seen him kill. No way could she tell Chas about Lady Rachel. She knew she should feel sad, but she just felt numb. Perhaps that's how your mind goes when there's just too much to take in at once. Her thoughts kept returning to Lady Rachel's car, parked out front for all the world to see, come morning. How long before someone made the link between it and the old bag lady lying dead in Rats' Alley? And then they'd get Chas in to identify the body. And Joseph would tell him how Lady Rachel had left the Spotted Cow with Nick . . . If Nick was arrested, there'd be no one to protect her against the danger that still lurked out there in the darkness.

She waited until she was sure Chas was sleeping soundly, then she crept up the stairs and outside.

Lady Rachel never locked her car. Her philosophy had always been that she had nothing worth stealing, nothing she would miss. If a thief was that desperate, he was welcome to what he could find inside. She had, however, taken the keys from the ignition.

Luckily, Park Road was on a slight slope. Jools opened the car door, took hold of the steering wheel with one hand and began to push. As soon as she'd got up a fair speed, she jumped in, pulled the door to behind her and let the car coast. She kept her foot resting on the brake, just in case she had to make an emergency stop, but the streets were quiet at this time of night. She made it to the end of the road and turned the corner without slowing down. Gradually the road flattened out, but the car kept going. She must have come a good three-quarters of a mile by now. Ahead and to the left there was a small parking area outside a church, tucked in behind a row of terraced houses. You could leave a car there for days and no one would notice – especially with a load of jumble in the back. Church ladies were always collecting for something.

She shut the car door quietly as she got out and took a quick look round to make sure she hadn't been seen.

There seemed to be no one about, but she hadn't taken more than a dozen steps back the way she'd come when she felt that odd prickling up the back of her neck which told her she wasn't alone in the street.

Another quick look round. Nothing moved, except for the gentle swaying of the trees lining the road, which made their shadows shift and dance.

She walked on, stepping out smartly, head up. *I know where I'm going, don't mess with me!*

Whoever it was, was getting closer, she could feel it. Nick, playing tricks? It had to be.

She swung round, calling out, 'Nick?' and found herself face to face with Professor Hollander.

'Miss Julie! Did I frighten you?' Head tilted to one side, lamplight reflecting off his spectacles, he scolded her gently. 'If I have frightened you, this is partly your own fault, I think. Young women should not be wandering alone at such a time. Permit me.' He took her arm. 'I will escort you home. This way.'

She glanced back up the hill, the way she'd come. It suddenly seemed insurmountable. If the Prof knew a quicker way, then she'd better take it.

He led her through a dark passageway between blank, crumbling walls, explaining that this was a short cut that would bring them out at the back of the house. There was a door there into the garden. 'You are tired, my dear.'

Too right. He wasn't such a bad old stick. Not his fault if his wife running off like that had turned his head a bit. They were walking through the oldest part of town. Front doors opened straight onto the pavement from Elizabethan half-timbering, Georgian neo-classical and Victorian terraces, then came something that might have been an old coaching inn, with a wide arched gateway. Through it she could see a development of brand-new maisonettes. Lights shone dimly through drawn curtains in bedrooms and in a few downstairs rooms she caught a glimpse of flickering television screens. It was very quiet. They saw not a living soul, apart from a stray dog that crossed the road ahead of them.

Then they were in an avenue, houses set back on either side, cars tucked well out of sight. The year might have been 1796, 1896–1996 seemed the least likely option.

The Prof was walking faster now. He was breathing heavily, as if he was in a hurry to get this over with, so he could be somewhere else. Jools said, 'If you've got things to do, you can leave me here, just point me in the right direction.'

'No, no. I must not lose you.'

'I won't get lost. It can't be far now.'

'Not far. Not far!'

She looked for the church spire. If they were heading back towards the house, it should have been behind them, but it was over to the right. It wasn't like her to have lost all sense of direction. She didn't know this part of town at all. They were coming out into a square of Georgian town houses with a railed garden in the centre.

'This way,' he said, drawing her into the garden through a little iron gate.

'This way?'

'It is a short cut,' he insisted. They ploughed on, fallen leaves muffling their footsteps. 'Not long now.' Suddenly he stopped and turned and looked at her. 'You must not be afraid.'

'Afraid?'

'My dear, I am so sorry. For your father's sake, I am so sorry!'

'Sorry for what?' Alarm bells were suddenly ringing in her head.

Bushes and trees screened them from the houses all around. Ahead, moonlight shone on a fountain, with a statue of Pan, the basin choked with dead leaves.

Half to himself, the Professor went on, 'I have tracked him for so long, searching for the place where he hides by day. Night after night, through these dark streets, I follow – and then, each time, he is gone! Leaving behind him another victim.' He caught hold of her arm. 'I do what I can for them.'

Keep calm, Jools, she told herself. Wait for a chance to break away, out of the shadows and into the light . . .

'What can you do for them?' *Show an interest. Keep him talking.*

'I can save them from the worst fate of all. It is a terrible thing,' he said earnestly, 'to be undead. To wander always between life and death. Like my poor Liesl.'

If she could make a dash for it, into that little patch of light, and scream and scream . . .

'I failed her!' he cried.

She twisted her arm, trying to force him to let go, feeling the panic rising inside her as his grip tightened, yelling at him, 'Let me go! Liesl is not undead, you stupid old man! She's living in Clacton-on-Sea!' She wanted to laugh. She wanted to weep. What she had to do was run . . .

She felt the seam tear as she wrenched her arm free of the sleeve. At once, he had her by the hair, jerking her head back.

'Miss Julie, I have warned you – tried to protect you. It seems that the cross, after all, is no protection. Perhaps, if one does not believe . . . This I must investigate further . . . record in my notes . . . So, I have seen you with him – touch him – kiss him! The vampire! You are lost, Miss Julie! This I do now is for your own good! Better to be dead than one of the undead!'

She saw the flash of the knife raised above her and heard a kind of cry of protest, more like a death-rattle, that must have come from her own throat. Then a shadow – a whirlwind – passed between her and the knife and there was a shower of blood. Blood everywhere: was this what it was like to die?

Dimly she heard Nick's voice, shouting, as if from a great distance, 'Get out of the way, Jools, damn you!'

How could she, with her hair still tangled in the old man's fingers? Then there was a *crack* of breaking bone and the arm holding her went limp. She struggled free and, crouching, saw above her the knife striking downwards, again and again. Nick's left arm came up to block it, while his right whipped round to clutch and twist the wrist that held it. Another sickening *crack* – and the knife fell uselessly upon the ground, leaving the Professor poised, looking after it, both arms hanging limp, before Nick spun him round, his still-good arm round the old man's neck, while his knee came up into the small of the back. With one quick jerk it was done, the spine broken.

Nick let the lifeless body slip from his hands to the ground and would have followed it, if Jools hadn't caught him and helped him to a bench.

There was blood everywhere – the smell of it! – over Nick's coat and shirt and face; over her clothes, too, as well as on the ground.

His first thought was to ask her, 'Are you hurt?'

Quickly she checked. 'No, not a scratch. But what about you?'

He looked terrible, paler than usual, if that was possible. There was a deep gash down his cheek, another on his left forearm, to judge by the mess made of his coat, but the worst damage was to his left shoulder, the blood soaking his shirt, spreading as she watched. Gently she moved the cloth aside, easing it away where it was caught in the wound. Blood followed it.

'I got in the way,' she murmured. 'I'm so sorry!'

'I'll mend.' He forced a smile. 'I'm a vampire, remember? Neither living nor dead. By this time tomorrow I'll be as good as new. That's not to say it doesn't hurt like hell.'

'Should I – call a doctor?' she offered.

'There's nothing any doctor could do.' His smile turned to a grimace. 'Lucifer! Strange, isn't it, how you forget pain until you're hurt again?'

'There must be some way I can help.'

'Sit with me till the bleeding stops. Then I'll be ready to move.'

She sat down beside him, comforted to feel his right arm sliding round her. She looked down at the Professor's body. 'It was him,' she said shakily. 'He killed those girls.'

'With the very best intentions. Saving them from a fate worse than death. Silly old fool! If every time a vampire fed he created another vampire, the world would be full of us by now, all immortal, all feeding off one another, nothing else to do, nowhere to go. That would be hell indeed.' He rubbed his head against her and said softly, 'You have to give your soul, Jools. Without that, we two could drain each other dry and it would make no difference.'

She couldn't stop shaking. 'I was nearly number five.'

'I would never have let him hurt you.'

'You knew it was him?'

'I thought it possible.'

'Since when?'

'Hard to say, really.' He reflected. 'With each one I became more certain. If I'd known from the start that losing Liesl had sent him completely off his head, I might not have . . .'

He seemed on the point of falling asleep.

'It has been fun, though, hasn't it?' he murmured. 'I thought it would be fun to put the three of you together.'

'You *what*?'

'Just dropped a hint or two. Josie did the rest. Chas and the Prof, I thought they'd be company for one another. Comparing notes. Reviving old memories.'

The idea took her breath away. 'Oh! That was cruel.'

'I can be very cruel.' He didn't care. 'I thought it would make things more interesting. You've no idea how boring immortality can be.'

'You used me as bait!'

'I'm sorry,' he said, so meekly that she couldn't bring herself to go on being angry. Then his mood changed again, to one of elation. 'Admit it feels good, though! To come so close to death and find yourself alive! I would never have let him hurt you. I was the one who got hurt. It hurts,' he said plaintively. 'Take me home now. I want to go home.'

'Is it far?'

'Not far.'

CHAPTER TWELVE

The house was only just round the corner, but they made such slow progress that she wondered if they'd ever make it. She kept her arm around him as they went, trying to support him, but it was the sudden spasms of pain that slowed him down, rather than weakness from the loss of blood, and there was nothing she could do to help, except be there. Moonlight shone softly on railings and on white buildings, with dark, shuttered windows. They moved as if in a dream through a world asleep. At last they reached the door.

'Keys in my right pocket,' he said. 'No one to hear us. Old lady downstairs – deaf as a post. First floor: an accountant's office and a dentist's. No one gets into either of them without using the entry-phone. Upstairs – just me. The perfect hide-out for a vampire.'

'Shut up, Nick. Just keep moving.'

They climbed upwards one step at a time, blood oozing again from his shoulder, running down his arm, drip, drip, drip on every stair. A one-eyed man could track them. But first someone had to find the body and call the police. They were probably safe till daylight.

'The other key.' Nick nodded.

She pushed open the door and helped him inside. She was astonished by the ordinariness of the place, a living-room with TV and stereo, shelves of books, one or two good pictures; a modern kitchen (unused), bathroom, bedroom – the bed, complete with duvet.

'No coffin?' she asked.

He grinned. 'That idea belongs to a time before decent locks were invented. So long as I keep the daylight out,' he pointed to the wooden shutters on the windows, 'why shouldn't I sleep in a bed, like anyone else?' He sank down on the edge of it. 'Take off my shoes and socks.'

She kneeled and did as he asked. His feet were perfect as a statue's, slender and smooth.

'Mm!' he murmured. 'That's nice. Go on rubbing my feet.' He gave a deep sigh and stretched out on the bed, closing his eyes. 'Don't let me fall asleep. I must be gone from here by morning.' She caught her breath. *So soon?* 'The danger's past; there's nothing to keep me here now. Besides,' he went on patiently; 'there is a body in the garden, with a trail of blood leading directly to my door. The police are bound to start asking a lot of boring questions. So, are you coming with me?'

Jools bit her lip: she still couldn't make up her mind. She said quietly, 'I talked to Chas about my mother. Why was she so afraid of you?'

'She was different from you – not so independent. Not so strong.'

'He told me how she died.'

'Not my fault.'

He said it so dismissively that she burst out, 'I thought you said you loved her?'

'I did, while she was alive. It was a long time ago.'

'Four girls have died in the last month because of you. Aren't you the least bit sorry?'

'Dead is dead. Sorry won't bring them back.'

'But if you hadn't . . .'

'Oh, if, if, if! If ifs and ands were pots and pans . . .! How I loathe the smell of dead blood! Help me get these stinking clothes off. I'm going to take a shower.'

She had to fetch scissors to cut away his jacket. Underneath, the shirt was stuck fast to the wound with congealing blood.

'I'll get some water,' she said, after trying unsuccessfully to ease it free.

'There's water in the shower,' he snapped. 'I'll soak it off in there. Find me some clean clothes. Better take something for yourself, too,' he called over his shoulder. 'I shan't be needing any of it.'

Barefoot, dressed only in his shirt, he still moved as gracefully as a dancer.

Soon she heard the shower running.

Looking at herself in the mirror, she saw that there was blood on her hands and face and in her hair. Lady Rachel's jacket, blood-soaked and torn apart, was ruined beyond repair. When she took it off, she found blood on her shirt, too. She cleaned herself up

213

at the kitchen sink as quickly as she could and, while she towelled her hair dry, riffled through the clothes in the wardrobe, picking out a white silk shirt – highly impractical, but like cool fingers stroking her skin – and a black suede jacket.

After she'd done all that, she could still hear the water running in the shower.

'Nick?' she called. 'Nick, are you all right?'

No answer.

She pulled back the curtain and found him slumped on the floor, eyes closed, his head resting against the tiled wall, the blood-soaked shirt trailing from his hand, pale as the Christ in a pietà, as beautiful, and as perfect.

Jools turned off the water and, reaching for a towel, began to dry his hair and face. The gash on his cheek was already no worse than a scratch from an angry cat, the cut on his forearm mending almost as she watched. Only the wound in his shoulder still gaped open, like a jeering, toothless mouth. The more she dabbed at it with the towel, the more freely the blood seemed to flow. She wiped it quickly from her fingers. Blood of a vampire.

Then she saw that his eyes were open, watching, mocking. 'You mortals!' he murmured. 'How many times do you have to be told? You can't become a vampire by mistake. You have to be ready to give your soul, Jools. That's why there are so few of us. Now, help me up.'

Obediently, she wrapped a bathrobe round him and helped him back into the bedroom and onto the bed. 'How does it feel?' she asked.

'It feels pretty good.' He winced.

'It still hurts?'

He gave a mirthless laugh. 'Of course it hurts! It's good to feel pain sometimes. The pain *and* the pleasure, that's what makes life worth living. Eternal bliss! Who wants it? Now I've got you.' His good arm reached up so he could stroke her hair. 'You will come with me, won't you?' She felt his hand on her back, drawing her gently towards him. 'If I'd known there were only sixteen more years to wait . . . I'd never have bothered with her.' His voice was sweet as music playing inside her head. 'It's you I want. I feel so weak! Must have lost more blood than I thought.' Taking hold of her wrist, he gently pushed back the sleeve. 'May I? See?'

he said softly, smiling up at her. 'I remembered to ask this time.'

To ask, but not to wait for an answer. She felt a brief, sharp pain as his nail pierced the skin. Then he was drinking, totally absorbed. Drinking her blood. She didn't mind. Any healthy person can spare a pint. A pint? Almost an armful! She grinned to herself: Chas would have got the reference at once. Once Chas had woken her in the middle of the night so that she could watch a litter of puppies being born. Afterwards, their first instinct had been to suck, like this, before ever their eyes were open or their mother had any milk for them to drink. Chas would remember . . .

'Don't think about Chas,' Nick murmured. 'You don't need him any more. You think you owe him something? You'd never even have known him if it hadn't been for me. He'd have been long gone by the time you were born. It's what he does, isn't it? He always leaves them before things get too heavy. In the end, he would have left her anyway. The only way she could keep a hold on him was to die. He'll never be free of her now.'

'Poor Chas!' she whispered. Poor Chas. Dragging his guilt around with him through all those years. Like the Ancient Mariner.

'Let him go,' Nick whispered. 'It's you I want. Your memories . . . Not his.'

But Chas was part of every memory: books they'd read together, films, jokes. A name, a look, even, was enough. She only had to say to Chas, 'Remember Harrogate?' And she knew he'd remember the same afternoon: tea in a posh hotel (heaven knows what they were doing there) and a string trio of elderly ladies playing in the background. After a while she'd leaned over to Chas and whispered, loudly enough for everyone to hear, 'Are they going to go on making that noise all the time?' She'd been so young she would have forgotten, if Chas hadn't recalled it years after. Then she remembered how afterwards she'd sat entranced by the sight of the knee-length salmon–pink bloomers the cellist was wearing under her cocktail dress. She'd never told Chas that bit. Their memories were the same, but different. Memories shared, not stolen. And she knew then that she wouldn't be leaving with Nick.

He must have sensed that he was losing her. 'I would have taken you both!' Nick urged. 'Your mother and you. Looked after you both! Given you both anything you wanted!'

'The world on a plate,' Jools said slowly. 'So you could suck it out of her, drop by drop, every sensation, every thought, every emotion! And when you'd drained her dry and spat her out, you would have started on me. No wonder she was terrified.'

He flinched, as if she'd slapped his face. 'I've lost again, haven't I?' he said quietly.

She stared at him. 'Is that all this is to you? A game of winners and losers. And you hate to lose. That's why you came back for me.'

'No!' He was fingering her hair again, arranging it strand by strand to frame her face, as if etching her portrait in his memory. 'I want you,' he said miserably. 'I need you. I can't feel things the way mortals do! Nothing changes me. I'm so alone.'

At last; the simple truth. Too late. How long before he began again, cheating, lying, manipulating, like any spoilt child?

'You're used to being alone,' she answered. 'You can handle it.'

He held her gaze. Then he sank back on the pillows. 'Go on, then.' He waved a dismissive hand. 'Off you go. Go home!'

The suddenness of it took her by surprise. It was on the tip of her tongue to say, 'Wait a minute! Let's talk some more.'

Instead, 'We've got to get you dressed,' she said, 'and out of here.' Think of yourself as his nurse, she told herself. There was no first-aid kit in the flat. Nothing. Feeling like some Victorian heroine, she tore a shirt into strips to pad the wound at his shoulder and bandage it. *But he's going away. By dawn he'll be gone – must be gone. Remember him! The glow of his skin; the shimmering highlights in his hair; those sea-green eyes, with a sadness deep enough to drown in and never cry for help!* His sudden shifts of mood, constantly catching her off-balance – life would be dull, dull, dull! without him.

Like a sulky schoolboy, he was giving her the minimum of help, standing up, sitting down, raising an arm, letting her fasten buttons and zips, then at the end of it all, broke into a cheeky smile, 'You're like a mother to me, Jools.'

She tried to keep a straight face. 'You never give up, do you?'

Think of the police. Think of the danger if he's locked in a cell. Sun burning that smooth, white skin. Scientists standing in line to cut him up, to watch and see why he heals so quickly.

'Time to go,' she said, and stood up, hoping her legs would be a bit steadier than her voice. She picked up the bunch of keys. 'Where's your car key?'

'Haven't got one. Haven't got a car. If I need one, I just borrow one.'

'You mean steal?' she demanded, as they set off down the stairs.

'I always give them back.' Standing at the top of the front steps, he looked optimistically up and down the road.

He was impossible. Jools told him firmly, 'You can't risk being picked up driving a stolen car. We'll have to use Lady Rachel's. This way.' She led him back the way she'd come with the Professor, remembering it exactly, centuries overlaid by centuries, nineteenth, twentieth, eighteenth, then an old coaching-inn, even older, cocooning a modern block of maisonettes, until they finally arrived outside the church. 'The only thing is,' she said, as they stood beside the little Morris Traveller, 'I haven't got the key.'

He laughed. 'My dear girl! I've been tinkering with cars since they were first invented. If I can't get this thing started . . .!' He lifted up the bonnet and peered inside. 'Ah! Here we are!' In less than a minute he had the engine going and was seated behind the steering wheel: too soon! Too soon! She didn't want him to go.

'Where will you go?' she asked him.

'Trust me. I'll find somewhere to hide up before daylight. In two hundred and seventy years, one develops an instinct for these things.' He drew her head down towards him for one last kiss. When she closed her eyes, there was no smell, no taste, no warmth, like kissing a ghost. As if he was already far away. 'Smile for me, Jools,' he whispered. 'That's how I want to remember you.'

As he turned away and fixed his gaze on the road ahead, he seemed almost to have forgotten her already.

She watched him drive off down the road, until the little red tail-light of the Morris Traveller was out of sight, wishing she could see the funny side and laugh at the idea of a vampire making his escape at a top speed of maybe fifty miles an hour, but feeling only a desolation she hadn't known since she was a small child, standing by the playground wall. Someone had stolen her little pink plastic elephant; her talisman; her lifeline to Chas. And she was the loneliest person in the world, sinking into a bottomless well of loneliness. She wrapped the black suede jacket – Nick's jacket – tightly round her and turned away.

At the first phone box she came to, she dialled 999 and asked for the police. She said, 'Your serial killer is in the garden in the middle of—' She named the square. 'There's no hurry,' she added. 'He's not going anywhere.'

She hung up before they could ask her for details of where she was calling from, her name and address. They'd find out soon enough. Then she went home.

*　　*　　*

In the kitchen she made a pot of tea and took a cup in to Chas and woke him. Then she sat down on the bed.

'I've got a story to tell you,' she began, 'about three vampires . . .' She told him everything. On the way home she'd decided that that was how it would have to be, because they had always shared everything, apart from that one secret about her mother.

At the end Chas thought for a long time, then he said, 'I should have believed her. If only I'd believed her . . .'

'You did the best you could,' said Jools. 'Who believes in vampires nowadays?' She paused. 'Nick said you would have left her. Would you have left her?' she asked.

Sadly, he shook his head: 'I don't know. I'll never know.'

'It's OK, Chas. You never left me. Not in sixteen years. Don't say you haven't been tempted, from time to time.' She kissed him, savouring the warm, human smell of him; the scratchiness of his chin. With her finger she traced the laugh-lines at the corners of his eyes, trying to remember how he'd looked before. If she saw a photo, of course she'd recognise him, but that's what it is to be human; to be always changing. *Poor Nick: never a day older – or different – than on the day he should have died.* Aloud: 'It's time to stop blaming yourself,' she said. 'Time to stop running. Why don't you play me something?'

'Now?'

'If it's not too early in the morning.'

If the young police sergeant with the choirboy's face was surprised to hear the strains of a clarinet playing 'Ain't Misbehavin'' floating up the stairs when Jools opened the door, he did his best not to show it.

'That's pretty good jazz,' he remarked, as she led him downstairs, 'for eight o'clock in the morning.'

'You think some other tune might be more appropriate?' asked Jools. '"Ding-dong, the witch is dead"? Tea?'

'What?'

She lifted up the pot and he grinned. 'Yes. A cup of tea would be very nice.'

She could see that he and Chas were going to get on just fine. Jazz? Yes, he loved jazz. Played a bit himself, as a matter of fact – just drums, he added modestly.

Jools grinned to herself: the jazz mafia. Beats freemasonry hands down. Just throw a few names into the conversation: Bechet, Mulligan, Brubeck, Bird, Lady Day, and a murder investigation can take care of itself.

It wasn't even what you'd call a murder, since the victim himself was guilty of at least four. They had the Professor's diary to prove it. More a case of rescuing a damsel in distress, then. Jools found herself fitting into this role without too much difficulty. Yes: Nick had saved her from certain death. Yes: she'd phoned the police. Then she had come home: it seemed the sensible thing to do. What about Nick? She shrugged: he'd said he was going away . . .

The old lady in the downstairs flat gave him a glowing reference: such a polite young man! Such a pity about the rare skin condition that prevented him from going out in the sun! She'd seen a piece about that on the telly. But he was always willing, in the evening, to fetch her in a few groceries from the Indian corner shop.

Judging from the trail of blood he'd left, the police

decided he must be in need of medical attention. They checked the hospitals in vain.

While all this was going on, Chas and Jools moved in with Josie.

Mrs Hollander came back from Clacton-on-Sea to put the house on the market.

'Nick Fleming?' she said to Jools. 'Is that what he's calling himself now? Oh, yes, I remember! He gave me the courage to leave that crazy man I married to get my British passport. I shall always be grateful. Tell him that, if you see him.'

Life settled down again. Normal, routine, everyday. Jools patched things up with Meg, Meg changing her mind about Nick, who'd saved Jools's life, when all was said and done.

As for Joseph, he was turning into quite a piano-player, now they'd roped in young Plod to play the drums.

Chas and Jools were still living with Josie. No problems. It really seemed as if they'd finally found a place where they could settle down.

Then one day, towards the end of term, Chas was waiting for her as she came out of school, with their bags packed.

'What's this?' she asked him.

'Time we were moving on.'

'But I thought – what about my A levels?'

'Do those any time.' He started walking away. 'Stay here, if you want.'

She hurried after him. 'What about Josie?'

'If I stay any longer with Josie, she'll have me fattened up and baked into one of her delectable pies so she can have me for breakfast.'

'What about the band?'

'They managed without me before. They'll manage again.'

'What'll we use for money?'

He turned and grinned at her. 'Two of those journos paid me for an exclusive.'

'Two?'

'I gave them two different stories, neither of them the truth. I thought we might go south for the rest of the winter. Spain. Morocco, maybe. When the money runs out, we can always hustle the tourists.'

He handed her her bag. Without a word, she took it and trudged after him, towards the bypass.

Sometimes she wonders if she made the right choice.

Chas does need her.

What about Nick? Sometimes she gets the feeling he's not far away. She remembers his promise: 'I won't let anyone hurt you.'

One night a guy followed her. A big man, heavy breather, with a wild look in his eye. She was scared. The worst thing was not knowing what was on his mind – rape, robbery, murder, even. Perhaps just the buzz it gave him, knowing he'd got her rattled.

Then, suddenly, he wasn't there any more.

They found him next day, with his neck neatly broken, the body tossed over a garden wall like so much garbage.

Somewhere, she knows, Nick's out there, watching over her. Her dark angel.

Another Hodder Children's Book

OWL LIGHT
A W. H. Smith Mind Boggling book

Maggie Pearson

'I'm going to be a werewolf!' said Ellie.

Under the owl light everything changes shape. Ellie disappears at night-time. Could she really be the werewolf Hal dreads in his imagination?

The common is a wild, forbidden place, a place of mysterious sounds, home to threatened badgers and the haunt of intriguing neighbours . . .

COMPANIONS OF THE NIGHT

Vivian Vande Velde

A terrifying journey through the night draws Kerry to the stranger, Ethan, as they flee his vicious hunters . . .

But then the pursuers turn pursued and Kerry must choose where true danger lies – with her companion of the night – or his attackers?

A vampire seeking vengeance.

A gripping supernatural tale.

Another Hodder Children's Book

LOOK FOR ME BY MOONLIGHT

Mary Downing Hahn

Cynda has a new home – a remote inn, snow-bound, full of shadows – and a new family.

Lonely and desolate, she welcomes the company of a sinister guest. But who is the girl, pale as sea-foam, who haunts the inn? Can Cynda break the power of the vampire's love – and save herself?

Is the stranger's love a promise or a curse?

ORDER FORM

0 340 65572 0	OWL LIGHT *Maggie Pearson*	£3.99 ☐
0 340 68300 7	COMPANIONS OF THE NIGHT *Vivian Vande Velde*	£3.99 ☐
0 340 68656 1	LOOK FOR ME BY MOONLIGHT *Mary Downing Hahn*	£3.99 ☐

....

All Hodder Children's books are available at your local bookshop or newsagent, or can be ordered direct from the publisher. Just tick the titles you want and fill in the form below. Prices and availability subject to change without notice.

Hodder Children's Books, Cash Sales Department, Bookpoint, 39 Milton Park, Abingdon, OXON, OX14 4TD, UK. If you have a credit card you may order by telephone – 01235 831700.

Please enclose a cheque or postal made payable to Bookpoint Ltd to the value of the cover price and allow the following for postage and packing: UK & BFPO – £1.00 for the first book 50p for the second book, and 30p for each additional book ordered up to a maximum charge of £3.00. OVERSEAS & EIRE – £2.00 for the first book, £1.00 for the second book, and 50p for each additional book.

Name...

Address..

....

....

If you would prefer to pay by credit card, please complete:
Please debit my Visa/Access/Diner's Card/American Express (delete as applicable) card no:

Signature ....

Expiry Date..